A NECESSARY KISS

Without the least plan, Alexander forged into the circle of light and ordered, "Unhand that woman at once."

Perhaps it was the baron's commanding tone, or merely the shock of discovering they had captured a woman, but the dragoons complied with the order, stepping back from their captive. Freed, Valara flew at Alexander, and he took the trembling young woman in his arms. His mind reeled at the idea that Miss Rochelle was somehow involved in smuggling, but as his gaze met Waite's over her head, Alex knew he would do all in his power to save her from herself.

With a flash of inspiration, an idea came to him to explain their being on the marshes. He crushed Valara to him, then tilted her chin and kissed her firmly on her lips. To his surprise, she kissed him back . . .

ROMANCE

Books by Lynn Collum

A GAME OF CHANCE

ELIZABETH AND THE MAJOR

THE SPY'S BRIDE

LADY MIRANDA'S MASQUERADE

THE CHRISTMAS CHARM

THE VALENTINE CHARM

THE WEDDING CHARM

Published by Zebra Books

THE
WEDDING
CHARM

Lynn Collum

ZEBRA BOOKS
Kensington Publishing Corp.
http://www.zebrabooks.com

ZEBRA BOOKS are published by

Kensington Publishing Corp.
850 Third Avenue
New York, NY 10022

All Kensington Titles, Imprints and Distributed Lines are available at special quantity discounts for bulk purchases for sales promotion, premiums, fund raising, educational or institutional use.

Special book excerpts or customized printings can also be created to fit specific needs. For details, write or phone the office of the Kensington special sales manager: Kensington Publishing Corp., 850 Third Avenue, New York, NY 10022, attn: Special Sales Department, Phone: 1-800-221-2647.

Zebra and the Z logo Reg. U.S. Pat. & TM Off.

First Printing: April, 2001
10 9 8 7 6 5 4 3 2 1

Printed in the United States of America

One

"Who the devil is making all that cursed noise?" Captain Niles Carlyle angrily tossed the blankets from his tousled blond head and sat up on one elbow, peering bleary-eyed about the small cramped room of the house on the Rue de la Mort. Seeing the culprit, his tone grew deferential. "Oh, 'tis you, Major. What has you up and about so early on such a frosty morn? Are the Bonapartists again spreading those damnable rumors about Napoleon returning from St. Helena any day?"

Major Alexander Addington ceased his packing to pick up a letter which lay open beside his portmanteau and pass it to his junior officer and friend. "All is quiet in town for the moment. This is a personal matter. I finally received a response to my query about my family's whereabouts in *Roma.*" The officer pronounced the name as only a native of the city on the Tiber would.

Niles squinted at the missive a moment, then rubbed his eyes before he tossed the paper to the covers. "I had too much brandy last night. What does it say?"

The major took a red uniform coat from the small wardrobe and began to fold it with military neatness. "It's from Signor Perelli, the innkeeper where my family held rooms at the time I left."

"Ah!" Niles retrieved the paper and peered at it again. "It's written in Italian. Then it ain't the brandy.

That's a relief; thought my eyes were going. What news does he impart?"

"He tells me . . . that my father died over a year ago." Alexander stopped a moment to stare out the small window, a faraway look in his glistening brown eyes. It had been eight years since he'd said good-bye to his father on the shores of the Adriatic, from whence he'd embarked for the safety of England. His mother had been an invalid, and her passing had come as no surprise, but Alexander had never dreamed he wouldn't see his father again. He pushed the painful thought aside, knowing his concern now must all be for his sisters' safety. With no further comment, he returned to his packing.

Niles sat in tactful silence, giving the major a moment to gather himself. At last he said, "Sorry to hear that, old man. What of your sisters? Did the fellow have anything to say of them?" The captain sat up, alert for the first time that morning.

Alexander placed another shirt in his portmanteau, but replied, "All he knew was that they moved several times in the intervening years. Luckily the man had a fondness for my late mother, so he made inquiries. He tracked them to a small *pensione* at the edge of *Roma*, only to learn they'd sailed for England last autumn."

"Well, that's good news." Niles lay back down on the bed, propping his head on his uplifted arm as he watched his superior officer put his brushes in the bag. Addington's history was known by most of the officers of the regiment—English father, Italian mother, raised in Italy, then having to flee at sixteen for fear he might be found by the French and conscripted into the army. After two years at Eton, the major's skill at cards had allowed him to purchase his colors, and the rest was history.

"What are your plans, sir?"

The major stepped to a nearby shelf and grabbed his

kit, inspecting it to make certain it contained all his toiletry articles. "I am returning to England. There are only two places the girls could have gone—to our godmother, Lady Margaret, in London or to our aunt Mrs. Reed in Basingstoke."

Niles reached over and picked up the miniature of the major's siblings that lay on the table between the two beds. The small painting depicted two dark-eyed young girls with raven locks the same hue as the major's. "They are deucedly pretty little girls. But then this must be years out of date. How old are your sisters now?"

Alexander paused a moment, doing the calculations in his head. A startled looked settled on his handsome features. "Why, Adriana is four and twenty and Amy two and twenty. I suppose I have still been thinking of them as they were when I last saw them waving from the windows of our rooms. But that was over eight years ago."

Niles returned the brass-ringed painting to the table, then tossed back the covers, dropping his feet to the cold floor. "Well, sir, if you take my advice, you'll find them husbands as soon as possible. I've a sister of my own, and I can tell you they go from one catastrophe to another, believing themselves up to every rig. But, truth be told, they need a husband and children to keep them occupied."

Alexander made no comment, merely continued to retrieve his personal articles. He'd been so long parted from the girls, he didn't want to contemplate handing either one over to some other gentleman as soon as they were reunited. Perhaps he would take them on holiday. Brighton was supposed to be all the crack during the summer. They could have their Season next spring.

A knock sounded at the door and a young lieutenant with a scraggly blond beard stepped into the room when summoned. "Major Addington, you're wanted at headquarters, sir."

The major swore softly under his breath and tossed the cravats he'd been folding onto his bed. He missed his batman sorely, but Crawford had been mortally wounded at Toulouse some two years earlier. To Alexander's way of thinking, the man was irreplaceable. "I shall be there directly, Mason. Are there rumors afoot that something untoward is happening in the town?"

The junior officer resettled his black shako on his head as he was about to depart. "All's quiet, sir. I think it's something of a personal matter that requires your attention. A gentleman has come from London asking for you."

Alexander was suddenly curious. Except for several old school chums he hadn't seen in years and his fellow officers, there were no gentlemen he knew personally. His godmother, Lady Margaret, was widowed, and he'd learned his uncle, Arthur Reed, had passed away while he'd been in the Peninsula. Having been a rather dreadful correspondent over the years, Alex's only news had come from his godmother in England, who dutifully wrote him once a year.

He retrieved his own round hat with plume, then bid Niles good day and hurried to the house on the edge of the village of Lille that the British government had leased for the duration of the occupation. British residency in France would continue until the French paid the war indemnity of seven hundred million francs per the Treaty of Paris.

Nothing of any major importance seemed to be happening at headquarters. Major Addington strolled into the small square courtyard, where the officers present were milling about or casually speaking with friends. He greeted many in passing but had no time to talk. The corporal on duty directed him to General Sir John Cradock, who'd held the command of the Forty-third since '03. Alex knocked on the door, then entered when he heard the general call to him.

The room was rather small, but large windows looked out over a small pond where elegant black swans sailed about. The general stood near a window, his back to the room, but he turned as Alexander entered. "Ah, Major Addington, you are looking much recovered from your wounds."

Alexander's injures had been minor in comparison to many in his regiment, but one leg wound had been persistent and had required the surgeon's knife twice to heal properly. It had kept him lingering in France much longer than he'd wished. "I am again fit, sir."

"Very good, but that is not why I summoned you this morning. Pray allow me to present Mr. Jacob Fitzroy, a solicitor. He has journeyed from London with some rather important news regarding your future. I shall leave you to discuss matters in private." With that, the senior officer departed through a nearby door.

Alexander's gaze trailed to a rather round gentleman who rose from a chair near the fireplace. The man wore a stark black morning coat, black waistcoat, and black knee pants. The severity of his dress made his skin look pasty white, as if he were rarely out of his office in the daylight. Limp brown curls were crimped around his stern face.

"Your servant, Mr. Fitzroy." The major executed a crisp military bow, all the while praying this had nothing to do with his sisters.

The gentleman officiously cleared his throat as he drew his hands behind his back, making his round stomach protrude from the confines of his ill-cut coat. "I fear I bring grave news. Bartholomew Addington, Baron Landry of Landry Chase, expired in January at his home in Norfolk. Being without male issue, and due to the death of Mr. Marcus Addington, the second brother,

the title was destined for your father. Alas, I have
learned from Lady Margaret, Dowager Countess of
Wotherford, that your father is also deceased. Therefore it is my duty to inform you that you have inherited
the title and estates of the late baron." Then, as if to
dampen any undue exaltation the young man might
experience at such a windfall, the solicitor added, "Such
as they are, my lord. I fear your uncle gamed away most
of what he inherited."

"You have recently visited Lady Margaret?" Alexander
took a step forward, eager for news from his godmother.
In truth, he cared little about this legacy at the moment.

"I have, my lord." The gentleman quirked one
brushy gray brow at the young man's unexpected response. "She was in excellent health at her home in
London."

"Did she perchance mention my sisters, Miss Adriana
Addington or Miss Amy?"

"She did. Your eldest sister was wed last Christmas
Day to Viscount Borland, her ladyship's grandson, at
the home of Lady Margaret. Lady Borland and her husband are presently honeymooning in Italy. The younger
Miss Addington was wed in February at Bath Cathedral
to Sir Hartley Ross. They are honeymooning at her ladyship's castle in Kelso, Scotland, at present." The solicitor paused a moment before slyly adding, "Both
gentlemen are wealthy, and one might apply to either
for a substantial loan if one were so inclined."

"I think not, Mr. Fitzroy," was all Alexander could
mutter, stunned at the news of his sisters' marriages.
He failed to take note of the solicitor's profound disappointment at his statement.

The major stood reeling from the news. He knew
Lady Margaret to be a dreadful correspondent, but why
hadn't she felt it necessary to inform him of such monu-
mental happenings in his family? Had she been hoping

he would return to England of his own volition after Waterloo? He'd been a fool not to write and tell her of his injuries, but he hadn't wanted to worry her.

In truth, he'd considered going straight from France to Rome to search for his family, but the surgeon had advised against such a journey, and Alexander had lacked the discretionary funds to go. He'd sent every spare pound he had won or earned to his old friend, Sir Roger Howard, to bank in London in the hopes of accumulating enough to bring his sisters to England and provide them with a Season.

But it seemed all his efforts were in vain if Adriana and Amy were married.

"My lord," Mr. Fitzroy said, as he stepped forward, his hand extended. "Lady Margaret asked that I deliver this to you. It's from your sister, Lady Ross."

Alexander eyed the small box the solicitor held with mild curiosity. What had Amy sent him? He took the small container and lifted the lid. On a black velvet cushion lay the golden charm he'd given to his sisters so many years ago just before he left them in Rome. He smiled as the engraved image of the Goddess Minerva glinted up at him, and the memory of his two sisters waving good-bye from the *pensione* window returned. He'd spent what little he had left to purchase this necklace as a memento for the girls in case he never returned from the wars.

"There was a message as well, my lord."

The solicitor interrupted the major's memories. When Alexander glanced at the gentleman, he found the man looking at the ceiling, his wide brow puckered in thoughtful concentration. Fitzroy began to recite the message as if determined to say it exactly as Lady Margaret had.

"Her ladyship said Lady Ross insists you wear this

good luck charm so that you will find your heart's desire, just as she and her sister did."

Amy's message warmed his heart, and his throat tightened with emotion. He lifted the charm out of the box and watched it spin on the gold chain, seeing the goddess on one side and the Latin words for *wisdom* and *prudence* etched on the opposite side. He doubted it held any magical properties, but to honor his sister's wish, he would wear the charm. It would remind him of their innocent childhood days in Rome.

As he slipped the chain over his head and dropped the medallion down inside his regimental jacket, his thoughts returned to the other news Mr. Fitzroy had imparted, the death of his uncle. He knew nothing about running an estate, and now he had inherited one in financial ruin.

Mr. Fitzroy cleared his throat in an effort to recapture the soldier's attention. "Do you intend to travel to Norfolk immediately, Lord Landry?"

The title sounded strange to Alexander's ears. His father had often spoken of the possibility that one day he might inherit the barony and must do his duty to the people of Landry Chase, a place as alien to him as England had once been. But a country estate in a far-off land had been too remote to a young boy growing up in Italy to consider, especially a boy who longed to be a soldier. Until this moment, he had given the matter little thought. Everything in his life would change from this day forth. He was being forced into a world he knew little about.

"My plans are unsettled at the moment, sir. You say my late uncle's estate is depleted?"

Fitzroy nodded. "I fear the baron bled it dry, my lord. It will be years, if ever, before you see a penny from Landry Chase. The lands, while vast, are not being used in any productive way. Most of the tenant cottages are vacant and need repairs."

Alexander walked to the window and looked out on the rolling hills of France. His life in the army was over, but how would he go about replenishing a nearly worthless estate? Then he remembered Sir Roger to whom he'd been sending every spare quid for his sisters' dowry. The baronet had inherited his father's estate some years earlier. Hopefully, he would be full of good advice. Alexander would visit his friend first and see where his finances stood, then try to coax Sir Roger to come to Norfolk and begin to try to set things to rights—at least as much as he could with his present funds.

Remembering that the solicitor was awaiting his reply, the major turned. "I have matters I must attend to in London. Then I shall journey to Landry Chase. I assume the widow remains at the estate."

The solicitor's eyes narrowed. What little information he knew about the soldier before him had come from the late baron and his lady wife. Having an adventurer and gamester in charge didn't bode well for the estate that once had been one of the finest in Norfolk. The major was said to be just like his father, Hugh Addington, who'd refused an appointment to the clergy and gamed his way across Europe until he'd fallen into the clutches of some Italian female and married her. Did this young man think to mortgage the estates he'd just inherited? Fitzroy thought he must do his duty and give the young man all the bad news at once.

"Lady Landry still resides in the main house, along with her daughter and several of her ladyship's poor relations. There are no funds to repair the dower house, I fear. But I feel it my duty to inform you Landry Chase is entailed, my lord."

"Entailed?" Alexander's thoughts were still centered on his worries about meeting relations who had been estranged from his father years earlier. He didn't take the solicitor's meaning.

"Set up by the fifth baron, my lord, since all his sons had a propensity for games of chance. One cannot borrow funds against the entailed property."

In an intuitive flash, Alexander realized this man had a poor opinion of him. The solicitor saw a penniless soldier who would try to take what he could from an already depleted estate. Alexander's back stiffened. "I have no intention of borrowing against my inheritance, Mr. Fitzroy. My years of soldiering have not been entirely unprofitable. Pray inform my aunt I shall arrive at the estate by the first week of April. I should like to have the steward ready with the books upon my arrival. Also be so good as to inform Lady Margaret that I shall pay her a visit before I depart London."

"Very good, my lord." The gentleman bowed, then departed from the new baron. After closing the door, Mr. Fitzroy's face twisted into something of a smile. It seemed the new Lord Landry would be nothing like what the dowager was expecting. Landry Chase might once again be restored to profitability if the soldier invested his prize money back into the land. It made the solicitor lick his lips with delight.

The ballroom at Landry Chase echoed emptily as Miss Elaina Addington, standing in the middle of the parquet floor, called, "Oh, please, come and let us have a final go." She dimpled at her cousin. Unfortunately for Elaina, her pretty smile held little sway over females.

Miss Valara Rochelle shook her head, making her blond curls sway. "You know Aunt Belinda shall be returning from Cley any moment. She always reminds me it's my duty to keep you from such hoydenish behavior."

"Then I remind her the exercise helps me keep my

figure trim, and she agrees that is quite true. She lives in dire fear I shall grow plump before I wed." Elaina ran her free hand down her black skirts making the fabric pull taut against her shapely figure. Sensing that her cousin was weakening by the smile on her face, Elaina added, "Come, Lara, you know I am right."

"Very well, one last time." Valara came back to where her cousin stood. Positioning her feet just so, she arched her back, then called, *"En garde."*

The two épées came together with a click, the Spanish steel glinting in the morning sunlight that poured through the great oriel window at the far end of the ballroom. Within minutes, the button-tipped swords were flashing with all the zeal and expertise that the late Monsieur Rochelle would have asked from any of his male fencing students. Despite her black muslin skirts, Valara lunged and parried just as her father had taught her.

In truth, her cousin's skills were as yet not so honed. It took the fencing master's daughter scarcely five minutes before Elaina's sword was stripped from her hand. The épée skittered across the ballroom floor and came to rest in front of the entryway just as the door flew open.

Neville Rochelle, Valara's younger brother, stepped into the room. His pale blue eyes widened at the sight of the fencing blade rocking back and forth where it lay. Looking to where his sister and cousin stood, he called a hurried warning. "Aunt Belinda has returned, and something has her in a rare taking. If she sees these swords, she's like to play the devil with your plans to ride to the old church at Cromer next week."

The young ladies exchanged a worried glance. Then Elaina dashed to her sword. She snatched it from the floor and raced to follow Valara to the stand where the practice weapons were stored. Both fencers managed to stow the blades and remove their gloves and leather plastrons without the least sight of Lady Landry.

The dowager baroness, a large woman grown stout with years of idle discontent and disappointments, rarely moved anywhere in a hurry, but Valara and Elaina had scarcely managed to settle into two gilt chairs before Lady Landry stormed into the room. In the normal course of events, her ladyship might have thought to inquire why the girls were in the ballroom and not the drawing room, but this morning she was far too upset to give the matter a passing thought.

She breezed past Neville, making straight for her daughter and niece, her black mourning gown overly tight on her ample form. Unfortunately, there were no funds for such things as new mourning attire for anyone. Her ladyship waved a piece of paper in the air as she approached the girls. "My worst fears have been realized." She paused to look from one girl to the other. When all she received were quizzical looks, she continued, "Mr. Fitzroy, the baron's solicitor, has written to inform me that the Italian usurper intends to come to Landry Chase by April." With that final announcement, her round face grew pink with distress.

Valara eyed her aunt with surprise at the strange statement. The lady was not known for her fair or logical thinking. In Lady Landry's mind, she'd tolerated more than most females of Quality, what with a husband who drank and gamed to excess; therefore, fate owed her—but just what, no one knew. "Mr. Alexander Addington *is* the heir, Aunt Belinda. Did you think he would write and say he didn't wish to be the new baron and we might keep the estate?"

"Write! For all we know he's an illiterate lout, having grown up in Italy. Why, he's never even set foot at Landry Chase, and now he can come here and turn us all out if he wishes!"

Seeing her aunt was about to work herself into one of her weeping fits, Valara rose and slipped a comforting arm about the lady's plump shoulders. "No matter his upbringing, Aunt, he is a gentleman's son. He wouldn't do that. Besides, you have the right of tenancy in the dower house."

Lady Landry took a trembling breath. Then her face hardened and her mouth grew grim. "I am certain the rats, terns, and gulls that inhabit the place won't mind sharing their quarters with us. He's not likely to spend a groat on repairing the place, and that foolish bailiff, Bailey, won't lift a finger to do anything until the new baron gives him the word."

The trio of young people had done their best to explain to the baroness that she could no longer command things to her liking at the Chase. Elaina came to her mother, her pretty face almost as grim as Lady Landry's. The matter of a stranger inheriting their beloved home was one of the first things mother and daughter had agreed on in years. "Don't worry, Mama. We shall not be bullied by some foreigner. Besides, there is always the legacy from my godmother, Lady Harper."

Lady Landry shook her head. "Oh, but Agatha would never do anything so agreeable as to die and leave us in peace. She is likely to outlive us all, and then where will we be?"

The group grew quiet. In truth, despite Lady Harper's promised legacy to her godchild, they all dreaded her rare visits to inspect her young heiress's progress to adulthood. Lady Harper was an ill-tempered, cantankerous woman who always managed to keep the house in an uproar.

Neville, awkward in such emotional situations, fidgeted with the gold buttons on his morning coat. The former brown superfine had not taken the black dye evenly, but his aunt insisted he wear it for mourning so as not to shock the neighbors. At last he kindly offered, "Then forget about Lady Harper. Lara and I could write our uncle, the *comte*, in Paris. I feel certain he would take us in if the new baron tosses us out. I am Ouelette's heir, after all."

Lady Landry glared at the boy, then snapped, "The Rochelles haven't had a feather to fly with since that rabble in Paris beheaded the royal family. Not to belabor the point, nephew, but his letters are so rare you are not like to know where your uncle Philippe might be at this very moment."

The Comte de l'Ouelette had dashed back to France after Napoleon's rout at Waterloo. He'd taken the time for only a brief visit in which he'd drawn his niece aside to inform her he intended to try and aid the Bourbons' return to the throne. While that sounded like great loyalty to the monarchy, Valara was certain the gentleman was hoping to be rewarded for his efforts. Unlike many who'd lost their estates during the Reign of Terror, Ouelette's father had lost his on the gaming tables. There had been only one proper letter after his arrival in Paris.

Elaina took her mother's hand. "Never mind about the *comte*. This is our home, and we shall stay and face Uncle Hugh's son proudly. Having a stranger in the manor will be rather disconcerting, but, after all, it is a large dwelling. We need not spend any time in the man's company, for we are in mourning. Why, we might never see the fellow from one week's end to the next."

Her ladyship produced a handkerchief from the folds of her black gown and dabbed at the tears that slid down her cheeks. "You can be certain he is an encroaching fellow and will be expecting us to introduce him to all the best families of the neighborhood." A look of horror settled on the lady's face. "You don't suppose he will have a dirty monkey with him like that little Italian who is forever loitering about the market at Holt?"

"Aunt Belinda," Valara said, a touch of exasperation in her tone, "you are letting your imagination run wild. The organ-grinder at Holt is a gypsy, not an Italian. You must remember Uncle Bart's heir has been an officer in Wellington's army for some years. I think we need not fear he will embarrass us."

"Well, we can be certain he's a gamester just like his father. It's the curse of all the Addington men." Lady Landry was not willing to give an inch on the subject of Alexander Addington. At last gathering her wits, her ladyship looked at a small clock on the mantel. "There is no point missing our tea about matters over which we have no control. Girls, go upstairs and freshen up. Whatever have you been about to put your hair in such disarray?"

Elaina's hand flew guiltily to her errant auburn curls, but Valara resisted the urge to tend the blond tendrils that had loosened about her face during her lively bout of fencing. As her ladyship's eyes narrowed thoughtfully, Valara looked to her brother for help. He didn't fail her.

"I'm famished, Aunt." Neville stepped to her ladyship and drew her arm through his, distracting her from her scrutiny of the girls. Valara watched them depart, grateful his timely intervention had saved them from having to tell a Banbury tale about why they looked like they'd been chasing cows out of the home garden, especially when the estate hadn't seen a cow since Uncle Bart's final visit.

Neville's inane chatter echoed in the ballroom as he led his aunt toward the door. "Pray, did you meet anyone of interest in Cley, Aunt?"

"Not a single person worth mentioning. But Lady Frances told me Lord Westoke and his sister are back from London. We should invite them to dine before Hugh's son arrives and turns things topsy-turvy. I would rest easier if things were settled between Elaina and the earl. 'Tis fortunate black becomes her. We are such long standing friends no one will think it improper for us to entertain him so soon after the baron's death."

"An excellent suggestion—if his lordship has forgiven Ellie her little escapade," Neville said.

"Bah, that was years ago. He will do his duty," the dowager stated emphatically.

Neville and Lady Landry disappeared into the hallway. Her aunt's final comments worried Valara, and a slight frown appeared on her brow as she eyed her cousin. In a low voice, she asked, "Do you truly wish to marry the Earl of Westoke?" She had never discussed the gentleman with Elaina, but Valara found the man a bit shallow and mean-spirited in his dealings with others. He'd been positively horrid after the incident with his sister at the hunt two years earlier, blaming Elaina for Lady Blythe's riding to hounds and her subsequent injury.

Elaina shrugged and avoided her cousin's gaze by staring out the window. "I must marry someone. He is wealthy and handsome. It was the wish of our fathers." Glancing back, she saw the look of disapproval on her cousin's face. Tossing her auburn curls, Elaina shook her head. "I cannot afford to be romantic, Lara. You see what that did for my mother and yours. Each followed her heart, and look where it got them—one married to a penniless émigré and the other to a wastrel baron. Besides, with Father's death we are at the mercy of this major we know nothing about. He may do as he pleases as the heir."

Valara couldn't deny the truth in what her cousin said about their mothers or the new baron. Valara and her brother were in greater danger than Aunt Belinda and Elaina of being asked to leave. They were penniless relations of Lady Landry with no ties to Landry Chase at all save their aunt's kindness, if one could use such a word about the baroness.

Valara's shoulders sagging, the orphaned woman moved to the window, gazing out at the unkempt garden. Valara's brows rose as another possibility dawned. Looking over her shoulder at her cousin, who seemed lost in unhappy thoughts of her own, she said, "There will be little to keep him here once he realizes Uncle Bart sold off everything not entailed and the place will require a great deal of his attention. I don't think he could wrestle another guinea out of the estate if he tried. And as an army officer, I doubt he will want to put his limited funds into the land to try to make it profitable again."

Elaina's pink lips tipped into a smile. "I had given the matter little thought, but I think you are correct." A wicked twinkle appeared in her green eyes and gave her cousin pause. "Perhaps if we are especially inhospitable to him, he will hasten his departure."

Valara frowned. "I don't recommend such behavior. You would only risk his—"

But the headstrong Miss Addington rarely listened to her cousin's advice. She tugged on Valara's arm. "I would never be openly rude to the man, so don't pucker your brow at me." She glanced at the clock on the mantel. "Come, we mustn't make Mama wait for her tea. She will be dreadfully cross."

When is she not? Valara thought, then pushed the unkind thought from her mind. Without her aunt, she and Neville would long ago have been forced into menial jobs. As she followed Elaina down the hall, Valara promised herself to broach the subject of her cousin's conduct to the new baron later, but for now, she hurried to her room. Aunt Belinda's mood was already too fractious. They mustn't add to the lady's annoyance by being late for tea.

Valara smoothed her blond curls back into some semblance of order, and her thoughts turned to the new baron. Her mind filled with questions about the man who would now control all of their destinies. Had he inherited the late baron's vile temper? Would he stay and try to turn things around at the estate, or merely look for what little might be sold from Landry Chase? Their future at the estate was no longer certain, and that frightened her. She would have to convince her brother he must be on his best behavior, at least until she again heard from Uncle Philippe.

Two

Upon his arrival in London, Alexander found the town in the throes of one of the greatest scandals to rock the foundations of the *beau monde* since the Duke of York's mistress had been caught selling military commissions and promotions. The separation of Lord Byron and his wife, Annabelle, had set the tongues of Society to wagging in February. By late March, the press became involved, printing every scurrilous rumor about the poet, previously the darling of England. His once adoring public began to turn on Byron when his wife's tales of an unnatural relationship between the poet and his sister were whispered throughout the city.

While the scandal appeared to be on everyone's lips, from the most elite of Society down to the bootmaker on Bond Street, Alexander had too many worries of his own to listen to the idle chatter and speculation. Having taken a room at the Pulteney Hotel in Piccadilly, he sent messages to Lady Margaret and to Sir Roger Howard, informing each of his arrival.

Within the hour, he received a note requesting he call at Hull House on Clifford Street, where the baronet resided with his grandfather, the noted Cit Thaddeus Hull. Alexander made his way to the less than fashionable address and knocked.

After giving his name to the aged butler and announcing his wish to speak with Sir Roger, Alexander followed the shuffling man down the small but elegantly appointed hall. He was ushered into the library, where the curtains were drawn against the morning sun and a fire burned in the fireplace. The stuffy room smelled of beeswax and camphor. The servant announced Alexander, then quietly exited the book-filled room, closing the door behind him.

At last Alexander's eyes grew accustomed to the darkened room and he realized the servant had made a mistake. Sir Roger was not in the library. Instead, Mr. Hull sat huddled in a leather chair before the fire. The shrunken old man was cloaked with a plaid rug; a talon-like hand clutched the woolen drape at his chest. A tuft of gray fuzz atop his head was all that remained of his hair. An assortment of apothecary bottles in varying colors sat on the table beside him.

"I am sorry, Mr. Hull. Your butler seems to have misunderstood. I asked for Sir Roger."

"My grandson's out. Ye ain't one of them high-in-the-instep swells what's afraid to even speak with a Cit, are you, Lord Landry?" The old man squinted at his visitor from beneath beetled gray brows.

Alexander couldn't help but smile at Mr. Hull's belligerent tone. "Not at all, sir. I'm just a soldier, and I've spent the last eight years mingling with some of the worst dregs of England. You might be more apt to fear what kind of man I've become after keeping company with the many pickpockets and thieves the courts sent to the Peninsula."

The old man's face relaxed, smoothing out some of the wrinkles. "I'll have Black count the silver after ye leave to be safe." Mr. Hull's chuckle turned into a cough. It took him several moments to recover his breath, and he gladly accepted the glass of water the baron offered him from the table.

While he drank, he gestured with his free hand for Alexander to be seated. Setting the glass aside, Mr. Hull again clutched at the rug, repositioning it on his shoulders. "Been sufferin' from an inflamation of the lungs this winter, but I'm on the mend. Roger wanted me to explain to ye about yer money, since he had an important appointment."

Alexander's stomach knotted. What had happened to the money he'd sent his old friend? Was it not safely in the Bank of England? Last night he'd taken the time to total the figures on the small notes he'd made over the years. He estimated he should have somewhere near five thousand pounds in the bank. He'd need every penny and more to put into Landry Chase if Mr. Fitzroy's report was true, and Alex had little reason to doubt the man. "Is there some problem, sir?"

Mr. Hull took another drink of his water, then smiled at his grandson's friend. "Don't believe so, but ye'll have to be the judge." Without waiting for any comment, he continued, "Back eight years ago, Roger came to me and told me that you had entrusted him with the task of depositing your money in the City. 'Twas I who convinced him to do otherwise." The old man, seemingly revived by talk of money and finances, sat forward in his chair, his face looking younger and less pinched. "Ain't no money to be made by sticking yer blunt with a bunch of boring bankers, my boy. 'Tis safe, but it ain't workin' for ye."

Alexander relaxed a bit. "That is true, sir. But I had no right to ask Roger to trouble himself with my finances."

The old man slapped a bony hand on his knee. "The boy takes after me, much to his late papa's distress. Sir Roger could turn a farthing into a Yellow Boy within a day if he put his mind to the matter." Mr. Hull grew quiet, and the smile fell from his face. "But it don't do Roger's standing much good to be rubbin' shoulders with the likes of me and my friends, and so I remind him every day."

"At Eton he was never ashamed of telling people you were his grandfather, sir."

The old man uttered a mirthless laugh. "Rubbed their highborn noses in it is more like. But we'll discuss my grandson later. What yer interested in is yer funds." Mr. Hull pulled a drawer open on the table, causing the bottles to clink together musically. He took out a ledger, which he handed to Alexander. "I started ye in something small that first year. Didn't have much to invest, but after several good profit turns, I purchased a small foundry for ye. The place was profitable within six months, so I invested yer new money in a tannery—but then, ye don't want me to be listin' every little decision I made. Had Roger write all the transactions down in the book."

The old man gestured at the leather-bound ledger with a thin, veined hand. "The long and the short of it is that after some buyin' and sellin', yer the owner of two profitable textile mills in Yorkshire. Got good reliable men workin' 'em. They'll produce a tidy profit every year if ye keep a close watch on your managers. As to the ready, ye got over forty thousand pounds in the bank."

Alexander's mind froze at the news. He blinked several times as the old man grinned back at him with smug satisfaction. Forty thousand pounds! It was a sum beyond a half-pay officer's wildest dreams. All his worries about what he would do with his depleted inheritance were behind him. With some good advice, he might turn the estate back into something a man could be proud to own.

Alexander knew he would never be able to thank the old man for his shrewd investments. "Sir, words cannot express what I am thinking. How can I ever repay you for what you have done for me?"

Mr. Hull sat back as his eyes narrowed in a look of cunning. Alexander was reminded of a fox. Clearly the old man had a favor to ask, and there could be no denying his request. He could only hope that it wasn't something utterly outlandish or time consuming, since there was much to be done at Landry Chase.

"Well, lad, it didn't start out that I was wantin' anything for my efforts. But as ye can see, I've been out of curl most of the winter. It's reminded me I shan't be here forever." The old man grew quiet as if thoughts of his own mortality were more than he could handle. His gaze moved to the fire.

Puzzled about what the old man could want, the new baron asked, "What can I do for you, sir?"

The hiss of burning coals was the only sound in the room for the next five minutes. Then Mr. Hull seemed to come out of his brown study with a vengeance. "Ain't me, but Roger I'm thinkin' of, *Lord Landry.*" The old man stressed Alexander's title.

"I would do anything to help my friend. I owe you both more than I can ever repay."

Mr. Hull smiled, again showing his age-stained teeth. "Then I want ye to invite him to this here estate what ye just inherited. Introduce him into the local Society. Help him find a blue-blooded wife, my boy."

Alexander was speechless. While he'd been fully prepared to do what he could to see that his sisters found husbands, the idea of being so presumptuous for his friend left him reeling. "Sir Roger is more than welcome to come, for in truth I should like to pick his brain about how to manage the estate, but I could never—"

At that moment, the library door opened and the man currently under discussion strolled into the room. Sir Roger Howard was a handsome young man with sandy blond curls he wore neatly brushed about a tanned angular face. He was of medium height, with a sturdy yet athletic build, but he owned none of the affectations that so permeated the gentlemen of the *ton*. His green morning coat fit rather loosely and his gray waistcoat held no distinctive pattern or ornate buttons. There appeared to be not a single fob or quizzing glass on his person and no jeweled stickpin in his simply tied cravat. The man was no slave to fashion.

"Alex, how good to see you." Sir Roger came forward and shook his old friend's hand. "Did Grandfather inform you that you are a man of means?"

Alexander owned Mr. Hull had done the job. The baronet took his grandfather to task for not having served their guest refreshments, and then ordered brandy and biscuits. The old Cit merely chuckled, saying he would leave the niceties of convention to his grandson. The men settled into chairs and briefly caught up on the years they'd not seen one another. Alexander learned his friend had prospered, as well, but as Sir Roger spoke of his activities in the City, he was forced to contend with his grandfather's grousing about his spending too much time at business.

Sir Roger arched one sandy-brown brow. "Since when did Thaddeus Hull begin to complain about earning money? I don't think it's your lungs that have grown weak, sir, but your brain."

The old man's eyes narrowed, yet bore a marked twinkle. "Mind yer tongue, my saucy lad. I can still lick ye in a business deal with one hand tied behind my back. But remember, I didn't struggle to lift my daughter above trade only to have her son sink back into the mire."

Suddenly Alexander wondered if the old man had told his grandson of the plot he'd devised to have his titled friend find him a bride. It wasn't something he would be willing to keep from Roger.

"Mr. Hull tells me he wants you to come to Landry Chase when I leave." Alexander watched the old man's response, but he appeared not the least bit fazed by the baron's candor. He merely nodded his head in agreement as he stared at his grandson.

Sir Roger grinned back at the old man. "Still think you can marry me off to some henwitted society chit if I will but go to the country where my Cit blood is unknown, Grandfather?"

"Ain't yer Cit blood I'm worryin' about, my boy. It's your refusal to attend a single Society affair here in Town. I don't want my grandson married to some counter jumper what's lookin' for a rich nodcock to trick into marryin' her."

Looking back at Landry, Sir Roger shrugged his shoulders. "Grandfather doesn't understand that any number of Society females could be mine for the asking. Money has a way of making one socially acceptable to penniless peers. But I don't want some lord who looks down his nose at me to sell me his daughter for the right price."

Mr. Hull snorted. "Don't be yammerin' about love and all that poppycock, boy. Ye find yerself a proper lady and produce some genteel offspring."

Alexander couldn't blame his friend for wanting more than a marriage of convenience. He'd seen too many such unions among the officers and their wives. Marriage without love too often proved to be misery. His own father and mother had risked the disapproval of both their families for love, yet had been happy in their poverty.

Alex knew he owed Mr. Hull for having taken such

limited funds and turning them into a veritable fortune. Still, the baron didn't want to be in the middle of a family argument. It was best to find a compromise in such situations.

"Come to Landry Chase with me, Roger. I won't force you to take a bride, but I could use your help and expertise. I understand from my late uncle's solicitor that the place has gone to rack and ruin. It seems I'll need every pound you and your grandfather earned for me to put the estate in order." Seeing Mr. Hull's brows move into a flat, disapproving line, Alexander added, "I shall introduce you to all the lovely ladies of the neighborhood, and you can have your pick—or not—as you wish."

The baron's statement did much to ease the old Cit's displeasure. "I'll not ask anything more of ye, Roger. Just go and visit with yer friend for a couple of months. Enjoy yerself and inspect the local ladies. Ye never know when ye might find the right one."

The young man looked down at the brandy glass in his hand a moment, then back to his grandfather. "I don't object to going with Alex, sir. But I don't wish to leave you alone with your health so indifferent."

"Bah!" Mr. Hull gestured with a swipe of his frail hand, but one could see by the twinkle in his gray eyes his grandson's concern pleased him. "I am on the mend, and well you know it. I couldn't even come downstairs two weeks ago. That old sawbones tells me I should be back at my warehouse offices by the end of next week."

Sir Roger eyed his grandfather a moment longer, then smiled. "Very well. I shall go, but you must promise if you have need of me you will write at once."

"I promise, my boy." The old man settled back in his chair looking more relaxed than he had in months, as if a load had been taken from his stooped shoulders.

The young men began to make plans for their departure. Sir Roger asked several questions about Landry Chase, but Alexander knew little.

Mr. Hull's beetled brows seemed to drop lower as he listened to the men. He leaned forward. "I should give ye a word of warning, Lord Landry. Ye've a fortune at your disposal to fix what ails yer property, but if ye take my advice, ye'll keep mum about yer finances. If there's one thing the gentry cannot abide, it's money made from trade, no matter that the man makin' it is a peer. It'll lower yer standin' for the source of the money to be widely known. 'Tis better to be thought a hardened gamester than to have soiled yer hands in trade."

Alexander nodded his head. There could be no denying that the taint of where his money came from would be damning with the local society in Norfolk, even though he hadn't directly engaged in trade. Not that he cared about such things, but he felt certain the dowager and her daughter wouldn't appreciate such an occurrence. He was already coming in at a disadvantage, knowing that his father's relations had shown little interest in him and his sisters. Their silence roared with their disapproval of Hugh Addington's offspring. Alex wouldn't do anything to add fuel to the fire. But he had a decided advantage—he and his circumstances were completely unknown by even his own family. He would keep his affairs private.

Sir Roger and Alexander agreed to depart for Landry Chase two days hence, giving the baron several days in Town to take care of both his business and personal affairs. He needed to replenish his wardrobe and purchase some horses.

As Alex made his way back to the Pulteney, he realized a whole new set of problems had come with his fortune.

* * *

Lady Landry tapped her slippered foot impatiently on the threadbare oriental rug in the green drawing room. She glared at Valara. "Where is Neville? You know how I dislike tardiness."

Miss Rochelle looked up from the pantaloons she was darning for her brother. "Have you forgotten, Aunt? He has his Latin lessons with the vicar every Wednesday."

Her ladyship sniffed. "I cannot think why you bother with further lessons since there are no funds to send him to Oxford. He would do better to—"

At that moment, the drawing room door flew open and a breathless Mr. Rochelle entered at a full run, then slowed to a more sedate pace. His light brown curls were tousled and a bit damp about his boyish face from a hurried washing up he'd just finished. "I do apologize, Aunt Belinda. Mr. Binion was late arriving because one of the boys was hurt while climbing in the trees at the orphanage."

Lady Landry's mouth flattened into a disapproving line. "The vicar pampers those homeless brats exceedingly. The older boys would be far better off in the workhouse, where they might earn their keep, than frolicking about the countryside becoming involved in all kinds of mischief."

This was an old argument that had always divided the Rochelles and Lady Landry. Neville and Valara could well appreciate the Reverend Mr. Binion's devotion to the young lads of Seaforth Orphanage, considering that except for their aunt's kindness they, too, might have been forced into the parish workhouse at an early age. The siblings knew their aunt's views and offered no disagreement with her opinion.

But Elaina was not so inclined. It often seemed to her cousins that she lived only to disagree with her mother. She closed the magazine she'd been perusing.

"Oh, Mama, what harm can there be in allowing the boys to stay at the orphanage until they are eighteen? The vicar, with Lara's help, has managed to teach most of them to read and write. They will be able to procure far better positions with such skills than they would from the workhouse."

"Shall I order the tea tray?" Neville offered, hoping to put an end to the thorny subject, on which they were not likely to come to a consensus.

Before the dowager could reply, the sounds of voices echoed in the hall. Lady Landry patted her black beribboned cap, squared her shoulders, then announced the obvious: "He is here." There was little enthusiasm in her voice.

All eyes turned toward the double doors, and there was a moment of breathless anticipation from all four occupants of the drawing room. The butler, Bainbridge, one of the few servants who'd loyally remained at the Chase despite the family's failure to make timely payments of salary, stepped into the room and announced, "Lord Landry, Sir Roger Howard."

Valara inspected the two gentleman with interest. Each was pleasing in his own way, yet there could be little doubt which man was the newest owner of Landry Chase. His Italian heritage could never be denied.

Lord Landry stood tall, well built, and fashionably attired in a well-cut green morning coat, green and white striped waistcoat, and tan buckskins. His raven hair was fashioned in a neat Brutus style about his olive-complected angular face. There was a wariness reflected in his golden brown eyes that belied his outward calm. He bowed and greeted his aunt politely.

His lordship's companion stood shorter and more broadly built, but still a very athletic-looking gentleman. He curiously surveyed the room, which was shockingly devoid of paintings, mirrors, and seating. Bartholomew

Addington's ravaging of the estate was evident everywhere one looked, from the nearly empty rooms to the worn and faded curtains at the windows.

Without a word to the gentlemen, Lady Landry instructed Bainbridge where to put the gentlemen's luggage. Valara, seizing the moment of distraction, squeezed her brother's hand and whispered in an undertone, "Remember, we must be on our best behavior with his lordship, but at the same time we mustn't anger Aunt Belinda, either." She'd discussed their precarious situation days earlier with Neville. If they were sent away, they could no longer be together, for the only respectable job she might find would be as a governess or companion. No employer would allow her to bring along her seventeen-year-old brother. He would be forced to work, but had no true skill to offer, since he lacked the patience to be a proper fencing instructor as yet.

Neville whispered, "Do you think he will tell us about his adventuring in the army?"

"Shhhhhhh," Valara hissed. "Not now."

As the butler departed, Lady Landry deigned to address her newly met nephew. "Well, sir, you have come at last to your family seat." The statement hung in the air like an accusation.

Lord Landry's dark brows rose in surprise. "Had I known you were anxiously awaiting my arrival, my lady, I would have come earlier. But then I don't remember ever receiving an invitation in the whole of my lifetime." There was heavy irony in his tone. All present were aware of the old family estrangement that had kept him from visiting.

The dowager's cheeks grew pink, but she offered no apology for any lack of hospitality. Instead, she turned her attention to Landry's friend. "Sir Roger, welcome to Landry Chase. I am surprised you were willing to give up the delights of Town during the height of the

Season to come and rusticate in Norfolk. I adored London and do so miss all the parties and other social events. It is my hope that once my daughter is wed, we can again live in London."

The young man bowed politely, but offered no smile. The lady's hostility to his friend lay like a pall over the gathering. "I could not allow the baron to face the wilds of Norfolk alone. Besides, I rarely attend such affairs in Town." A look one could almost call devilish came into Sir Roger's hazel eyes. "Perhaps because the grandson of Thaddeus Hull is seldom deemed worthy to be invited to such affairs."

"Hull, the wool merchant?" A look of horror settled on the dowager's plump features.

"The exact one, but wool is only one of his many ventures, Lady Landry."

The baroness's hands gripped the arms of her chair with such force Valara was surprised the wood didn't splinter. With an effort, her ladyship drew her gaze from the young visitor back to the new baron. "How long do you intend to stay at Landry Chase?" Her voice was as frosty as a winter gale.

Firmly, but without malice, he replied, "Aunt, this shall be my home henceforth. I must inspect the estate, for I understand much needs to be done."

The dowager's expression became indignant and she rose. "Well, you must see for yourself there is little to be had from this estate. In fact, one would need a king's ransom to put Landry Chase to right. You cannot say I didn't warn you. But you must excuse us, sir, for we are in deep mourning and not up to entertaining visitors." The lady signaled to Elaina, Valara, and Neville to follow her, then sailed past her stunned nephew.

Valara's cheeks warmed at her aunt's churlishness to the new baron. He was hardly a visitor in his own home. But she dutifully rose and followed the lady to her apart-

ments, keeping her eyes lowered as she passed the gentlemen. Upstairs, the door had scarcely closed behind
her aunt in the lady's sitting room when the dowager
vented her spleen as she paced back and forth in front
of the fireplace. "How dare he bring a Cit to the Chase
to embarrass us in front of our friends? I knew how it
would be. He hasn't a clue how to go on."

Elaina, who stood gazing thoughtfully into the fire,
remarked, "His grandfather is a Cit, Mama. That is
hardly the same thing. His father was a baronet."

The dowager turned on her daughter. "Cit or not, I
intend to see they are both gone from Landry Chase
within the month."

"We must tread lightly, Aunt," Valara said, attempting
to calm her agitated relative. "If you continue to be
rude to his lordship or his friend, he might well send
us all packing."

The dowager turned, her head held high. "He
wouldn't dare. He would be reviled by the neighbors
for such shabby treatment of a widow. I have given
the matter a great deal of thought. I am certain when
he sees we won't accept him into the family circle and
there is nothing for him to gain financially, he shall
return to his career in the army."

Valara thought the lady was being excessively foolish,
but it wasn't the first time her aunt's headstrong conduct had gotten the family into difficult waters.

Elaina stepped to the bellpull. "I shall order some
tea. That will calm all our frayed nerves."

None of them reminded Belinda Addington that the
neighbors well knew her ladyship's sharp tongue and
might not fault the man for putting a harridan from
his home. They all found seats to await the tea tray, but
silence reigned, each pondering the first encounter
with the new baron. Valara couldn't help but hope her
aunt would come to her senses. She was taking a great

risk. Yet despite the dowager's rude action, Lord Landry had conducted himself as a proper gentleman, and so she would remind the lady before they again faced the man that evening across the dinner table. She didn't want her ladyship's pride to cause them all to be expelled from their home.

Then her thoughts took an odd turn. There was nothing of the Addington family looks about Alexander Addington. In fact, he was a handsome man in a rugged sort of way. Valara sat up straight as she realized where her thoughts had moved. Her situation wasn't such that she could be having romantic notions about him—or any other man, for that matter. She would do better to spend her time trying to convince her aunt to behave. With that in mind, she set about doing just that.

Alexander stood in his shirt sleeves in front of the open window of his bedchamber and tugged at his cravat, loosening the knot with angry, jerky movements. The cool night air helped to draw some of the heat from his ire. His anger was equally distributed between his dead uncle and the man's annoyingly rude wife. But since Uncle Bartholomew was beyond punishment for crimes against the estate, most of Alex's indignation was directed at Lady Landry.

He was likely to throttle his aunt before many days were past if she didn't cease her barbed comments, hinting for him and Sir Roger to be gone since there was nothing left to glean from the Chase. The only thing that restrained him from giving the lady the dressing down she deserved was the memory of his lovely mother, pale and weak, asking him to make them proud. Over the years, he'd tried his best to honor that request, but his aunt was putting him to the test.

Dinner had been a strained misery for them all. Conversation had been left to Alex and Sir Roger, while the others had pretended to enjoy their boiled potatoes and mutton. The dreadful meal the lady had ordered didn't even bear thinking about. But Alexander had sensed a weakening in the wall of silence by the twinkle of interest in young Rochelle's ice blue eyes as Alexander answered Sir Roger's questions about some of his experiences in Spain. It was evident the young man was full of questions, but under orders not to converse with the new owner of the estate.

Tossing his untied cravat to the table, Alexander unbuttoned his shirt, then stopped to inhale the night air. The tangy salt smell of the nearby sea wafted on the breeze, helping to revive his spirits. Trying to relax and forget his worries about his aunt and the heavy burden of the depleted estate, he leaned his shoulder against the window frame and peered out at the landscape. Little could be seen in the inky night except the dark shapes of shrubs and trees, for the moon was but a sliver of yellow light.

Distracted by his tumbling worries, he fingered the gold Minerva charm he wore and thought about his sisters. He was glad they were off on their honeymoons and were not subjected to Lady Landry's odd humors. Her every word was a subtle condemnation that the son of an adventurer should have been gifted with such an honor as Landry Chase.

Honor! Ha! Clearly the lady had never seen the books the steward had brought before dinner. His late uncle had managed to bleed a once profitable estate to the edge of near extinction. Alexander knew it would take most of the money Mr. Hull had earned for him and the steady profits from the mills in Yorkshire to replenish the estate's depleted resources.

A knock sounded at the door, and Alexander called for the visitor to enter. Bainbridge entered with a tray on which sat a decanter of brandy and glasses. "My lord, I thought you might like to sample what the cellars of Landry Chase have to offer."

Alexander strolled to the table where the servant set the tray, picked up the brandy, and poured himself a small measure. "You mean there is something my uncle didn't manage to sell before he cocked up his toes?"

"French brandy is cheap in these parts, my lord. It wouldn't have been worth the effort." The butler took the crystal decanter, replaced the top, and put it back on the tray. He hovered a moment before clearing his throat to add, "My lord, I know I'm overstepping my bounds, but I hope you will be patient with Lady Landry and the rest of the family. They suffered his lordship's heavy hand as much as the estate."

Alex shook his head in frustration. "Despite what you all seem to think, Bainbridge, I am no wastrel, nor would I toss my uncle's family destitute into the world. I fully intend to put Landry Chase to rights, at least as much as my finances will allow at present. I cannot promise I won't move my aunt to the dower house once it has been repaired, however. That lady could try the patience of a saint."

At that, a hint of a smile flashed across the butler's face, but was gone in an instant. "Very good, my lord."

"Now that I have relieved your fears, do go and see if Sir Roger is still awake and would care to join me for some brandy."

"Very good, my lord." Bainbridge left with a jaunty step, despite his graying hair.

Alexander sampled the amber liquid while he waited for his friend. If nothing else, his late uncle had superb taste in spirits. He strolled back to the window. As he stood staring out at the park, a new feeling overtook him. Instead of being overwhelmed with futility at the task ahead, for the first time he was intrigued with the fact that all that lay within his vision and more belonged to him. It gave him a strange sense of power, yet at the same time a fierce sense of responsibility. Generations of Addingtons had improved and added to the estate before Uncle Bartholomew had wreaked havoc with his legacy. With the sea air blowing on his face, Alexander felt a strange connection with his roots that he'd never experienced during all those years growing up in Italy. He was home.

A knock sounded at the door, bringing the baron out of his revelation. Sir Roger entered, then poured himself a glass of brandy and joined his friend at the window. After a sip, the baronet grinned. He held up the glass. "I would guess this has never seen the tax man's stamp."

Alexander nodded. "Bainbridge just hinted as much, but it surprises me there would be much smuggling this far north."

"I don't think there is one inch of England's coast that doesn't see both the free-traders bringing in their booty and during the war the owlers taking theirs out on any given night. There is simply too much easy money to be made."

Alex nodded, then gave a half smile. "After looking at the books tonight, I may have to join the Gentlemen in their illegal activities if I'm to repair the damage my uncle has wrought."

The baronet knew his friend was only teasing, but in the spirit of the moment he again lifted his glass. "Then here's to moonless nights and adventurers."

The gentlemen clinked their glasses, then grew quiet as they enjoyed the contraband liquor. After several moments, Alexander glanced sidelong at his friend. "Why do you do it?"

"What?" Sir Roger asked, perplexed at the surprise question.

"Why do you insist on mentioning your grandfather's connection to trade to everyone you meet?"

Sir Roger sighed as he stared out at the rising crescent moon. "I learned a long time ago when you have a Cit in the family, it's best to inform people from the beginning. It spares one a rather embarrassing scene later on when the truth is out. I once had a young lady accuse me of despicable subterfuge for not telling her of my *tainted ancestry* as she called it."

That was something Alex could fully understand. He'd spent much of his adult life being known as the son of a ne'er-do-well adventurer. It had been one of the reasons he and Roger had been drawn to one another at Eton, being ostracized by the wealthy sons of peers. "What think you of my esteemed family?"

Sir Roger tapped his index finger on his glass for a moment. "The aunt definitely has to be moved to the dower house as soon as the paint dries on the renovations. As to the others, Miss Addington's something of a puzzle—one minute glaring hostilely at you with those amazing green eyes, the next hanging on every word about your experiences in the Peninsula. I would guess there is a great deal of spirit in your sedate little cousin. As to the Rochelles, I think the boy will be the first to crack and accept you, once you convince them you harbor no evil designs on the estate or their future. Miss Rochelle was so docile I could get no reading on her. In truth, I don't think she ever lifted her eyes from the floor or her plate. A pretty little mouse, I would guess."

"Her circumstances would allow for little else, especially under the domination of Lady Landry." Alexander realized the only note he'd taken of Miss Rochelle was when she arched her slender neck. Then she reminded him of the swans on the lake in Lille. His mind was too full of other concerns at the moment to have given either young lady much thought. They were both passably pretty females, and likely he shouldn't have much trouble marrying them off to some local gentlemen.

Sir Roger suddenly poked his head out the window. "Did you see that?"

"What?" Alex narrowed his eyes as he peered into the night.

"I thought I saw someone stealing toward the house. It was just a flash of movement, but I'm certain someone or something moved from that untrimmed hedge toward the front portico."

The two men stared intently into the garden. At last Alex straightened. "We cannot see a thing from here. I'm going downstairs."

He grabbed a candle and strode down to the front hall, Sir Roger on his heels. It took some thirty minutes to inspect all the doors and windows on the lower floor, but none were found to be open or unlocked. At last, standing at the foot of the grand staircase, Alex announced, "It must have been an animal. There is no evidence of anyone coming or going. Besides, you saw the rooms. There is little left a housebreaker would find of value."

Sir Roger's eyes still scanned the dark recesses of the great hall. "Perhaps it was my imagination, stirred by all our discussion of free-trading. You don't suppose one of the servants here at the Chase might be involved with the Gentlemen?"

The idea made Alexander's brow pucker. "If any are, I shall discharge them at once. I have enough worries without having to deal with that problem. It's one thing to joke about such matters, another thing to actually cross the line into breaking the law."

"From the few that are still employed, there doesn't appear to be a servant here under the age of fifty. It's not likely they would be so foolish."

"I hope that's true." Alexander turned and made his way up the stairs, putting the worrisome subject of housebreakers and smugglers from his mind for the moment. "Do you want to ride about the estate with me in the morning? The steward will be here at seven."

"I shall be ready."

The gentlemen bid each other good night at the landing. Returning to his chamber, Alex quickly changed, then settled into the four-poster.

But sleep escaped him. As worries whirled about in his mind, he decided once he returned from his morning ride, he must convince his newly met family he had only their best interests at heart. Maybe then they would quit treating him like some pillaging barbarian. Was it possible he and eventually his sisters would ever be accepted into the family from which they'd so long been barred?

Three

The morning ride round the estate was both exhilarating and daunting for Alexander. The Norfolk countryside was beautiful in the beginning throes of spring, with the colorful array of bluebells in the woods, yellow cowslips dotting the meadow, and pink lady's-smock fringing the salt marshes. The baron, Sir Roger, and Mr. Bailey, the steward, rode out with the intention of inspecting the dower house, which sat on the edge of the estate.

Yet there was little to see of good cheer for the new master as they cantered along. The pastureland they rode through held not a single sheep, cow, or horse. The tenant houses were in bad repair and standing empty. The fields lay fallow, no spring crops planted.

As they cantered over the wind-tossed grassland, Alexander could see the town of Cley-next-the-Sea across the wide salt marshes. The village was comprised of brick and flint buildings which reflected a decidedly Dutch influence from years of heavy trade with the Low Countries.

As the riders drew near the dower house which was designed to house the widows of the late barons, Alex's stomach sank. Facing the North Sea, the building had been ravaged by the salt air, wind, and time. The stone structure looked a mess, with the roof collapsed in one place and most of the windows shattered by the gulls and terns that found the crumbling house a safe haven from strong gales that blew off the water. Discouraged, he dismounted and walked through the building, accompanied by the others. Mr. Bailey assured his lordship that the basic structure was still sound. With a new roof, the whole could be repaired within a matter of months. Alex knew the restoration was an indulgence he could ill afford, considering the condition of the rest of the estate, but the thought of Lady Landry permanently at the Chase made him say, "Hire the workers and begin at once, Mr. Bailey."

By ten o'clock they'd seen scarcely a third of the estate, but Alex had pressing matters awaiting his attention at the Chase. He had hopes his sisters would come after their honeymoons, and he wanted the place livable. The men returned to the manor, making plans to inspect the remainder of the estate the following morning. Mr. Bailey hinted his lordship might visit the estate's mill if he had the time, then left to carry out the long list of instructions that had been discussed.

Sir Roger departed to change from his riding clothes, but Alex remained to summon Bainbridge to the library and take care of one thing he saw as a pressing need. The two discussed the requirements of the household. Then the baron issued orders for the butler to go to the nearest large town to replenish the depleted staff. While discussing the type and variety of servants needed, Alex reluctantly agreed to hire a personal valet. With details finalized, the baron urged Bainbridge to be on his way.

Alexander followed the departing butler into the front hall, inquiring about the whereabouts of his relations. As much as he might wish to avoid their unfriendly company, he knew things would never improve without such contact.

Bainbridge replied, "Lady Landry is still abed, my lord, as well as Mr. Neville, but Miss Valara and Miss Elaina are"—the old man hesitated a moment—"having a bit of exercise, I believe."

About to go upstairs, Alex stopped and listened intently to a faint sound that echoed from the depths of the house. "What is that noise?"

Without batting an eyelash, the butler said, "Rats, my lord."

That was a daunting thought. Men would have to be brought in immediately if the house was infested with rodents. The baron tilted his head and listened further. He arched one raven brow giving the servant a satirical smile. "And are the rats dueling to the death over the last piece of cheese? Bainbridge, I am a soldier. I know the sound of clashing swords."

The butler kept his eyes focused straight ahead. "Mayhap it's Cook sharpening her knives in preparation for tonight's meal."

Alex gave a soft chuckle. "Or to slit her throat after last night's offering? I think not." He strode in the direction of the sounds. He came to the double doors he'd entered the night before while investigating the nonexistent intruder and knew he was at the ballroom. He edged open the portal and halted at the sight before his eyes.

His cousin and Miss Rochelle, each swathed in a worn leather plastron to protect their bodies, were fencing with such skill, Alex stood speechless. He'd seen young officers in the Peninsula exhibit less expertise than these two females. He wasn't certain what amazed him more; females exhibiting such skill in gowns, or that it was the same two who had appeared so dull and spiritless in the dining room the night before.

Bainbridge cleared his throat. "I hope you won't tell her ladyship, my lord."

Alex continued to watch with fascination as the blades flashed in the morning sunlight. The two young women's faces were a study in concentration. "The less said to my aunt the better. That will be all, Bainbridge."

The butler looked as if he would say something more, but his gaze lowered to the list in his hand. Sighing, he said, "Very good, my lord. I shall go to Holt at once."

Alex pushed the door open and stepped further into the room to watch the extraordinary display of swordsmanship. It didn't take long to realize that Valara Rochelle was the teacher and her cousin, Elaina, the pupil. With every parry, the slender blond dominated Miss Addington.

Unfortunately, in the movement of her latest reprise, Miss Rochelle spied the gentleman and dropped her defenses. Elaina, unaware they were under observation, seized the opportunity to lunge forward with her épée and made a direct hit in her opponent's stomach. The buttoned blade struck the leather vest and forced the breath from Valara, causing her to fall backward on the parquet floor with a thud and lose her blade. She had barely hit the wooden surface before she gasped out, "My lord."

Elaina turned to view him, her green eyes widening with a mixture of horror and defiance. "W-we thought you would be riding the estate most of the day."

Alexander rushed forward, paying little heed to his cousin. "Are you unhurt, Miss Rochelle?" He extended his hand to her, then halted as he attained his first full view of her face.

The young lady held his stare with a pair of large blue eyes fringed with dark lashes. As he stared into their lovely depths, he was reminded of a summer sky. Blond tendrils had escaped her neat chignon and curled about her delicately carved features. His fingers tingled with the urge to brush the curls from her brow even as he noted the soft pink blush that rose in her cheeks.

Captivated by her lovely countenance, he found it difficult to believe this was the same little mouse he and Sir Roger had discussed the previous evening. It affected him deeply when he realized there was as much fear in her look as embarrassment.

In a gentle tone he again asked, "Are you unhurt?"

"I—I am not injured, my lord." She hesitated a moment, then took his hand and allowed him to pull her to her feet. The brief moment of contact seemed to only deepen her blush, and her gaze once again riveted to the floor.

"Lord Landry." Elaina stepped between the pair, her tone angry. "Why have you returned so soon? Surely you can see the estate needs your full attention."

Alexander dragged his gaze from Miss Rochelle to concentrate on what his cousin was saying. "I came to send Bainbridge to hire more servants for the hall. I thought you ladies might like to have a personal servant again. I understand there is at present only one upstairs maid for the entire manor."

Elaina tugged at the leather strap that held her plastron tied about her neck, but the ties resisted her efforts. "And just how do you, a half-pay soldier, intend to fund this luxury, my lord?"

A moment of stunned silence filled the ballroom. Alexander stared at the ill-tempered young lady. His every instinct was to give her a set down in return, but where would it all end if they kept one another at arm's length by forever tossing barbed comments back and forth? He might tell her the truth about his fortune, but that would only lower him further in his relations' eyes.

Managing to temper his anger, he turned to survey the near empty room and decided to go in another direction altogether. "Well, cousin, I noted any number of beautiful wildflowers in the woods. Perhaps I shall put the servants to work making bouquets to sell at the nearest street market, or perhaps we might take in washing and darning from the well-heeled of the neighborhood. If that fails to fill our pockets with blunt, I could sell the remaining furniture in the drawing rooms, since you and your family don't seem to make much use of it."

Elaina gasped in outrage that the estate would be brought so low, but Valara, taking note of the annoyed glint in the gentleman's warm brown eyes, suspected they were being roasted. Knowing Ellie's volatility, she put a calming hand on her cousin's arm, restraining her from making any more cutting remarks. "I think Lord Landry is saying that how he manages the estate in none of our affair, cousin. Is that not so, sir?"

"Just so, Miss Rochelle." Alexander's mouth tilted ever so slightly upward as he turned to survey the women. "You needn't worry as to how I shall manage my affairs. I promise there will be no more plundering of Landry Chase."

Seeing the skeptical look on Elaina's face, Valara hurriedly added, "It is very kind of you to think of our welfare, my lord, but truly we would not wish to put you to the undue expense of personal servants, especially when there is so much needed elsewhere."

Settling his gaze on the least prickly of the young women, Alex suddenly felt he was drowning in those blue eyes. With an effort, he drew his gaze to the wall of glass, which looked out onto an ill-tended garden, trying to gain control of his senses. "It is my wish to return Landry Chase to a properly managed estate, and that requires a proper staff, Miss Rochelle. I have hopes that when my sisters return from their honeymoon trips, they will come for a visit. I have not seen either in over eight years, having been away at war."

There was no comment from either young lady at the announcement. Alex turned to see each woman watching him, his cousin looking distrustful and Miss Rochelle appearing almost fearful. Was the young lady afraid of the changes he intended to make or of more unknown relations filling the Chase?

Only time could convince them he intended no harm to the estate or to their lives. Certain he couldn't win them over during a single meeting, he changed the subject. "I have rarely seen such a display of swordsmanship, ladies. I compliment you."

They exchanged a look Alex recognized as anxiety. Elaina took a half step forward. "Lord Landry—"

"Do you not think you could call me cousin, or at the least Landry? Despite being strangers, we are family, my dear Miss Addington."

Conflicting emotions ranged over the young lady's face. There was little doubt he was not what his family had expected or wanted. They were having a difficult time accepting a new baron, no matter that the old one had been something of a rogue. Finally she spoke. "Landry, about the fencing. I hope you will not find it necessary to mention you found Lara and me engaged in a lesson. My mother does not approve, and—"

Alexander raised his hand to halt her. "You need say no more. My lips are sealed. But may I enquire where you ladies learned to handle weapons with such skill?"

Miss Rochelle's chin rose a bit defiantly. "My father was French. He taught fencing to support us while we lived in London. I learned from a master and, in turn, taught Ellie, much to my aunt's displeasure."

"I am familiar with Lady Landry's wrath." Alex noted that they both blushed, but before either could comment, he added, "You have no need to fear I will betray you. Do use the ballroom for your lessons as often as you like."

Miss Rochelle gave a tentative smile. "Thank you, sir."

At that moment, a clock on the mantelpiece began to chime the hour, and the girls exchanged a look of horror. Miss Rochelle tugged on Elaina's arm as she exclaimed, " 'Tis eleven. We must hurry upstairs to change before Aunt Belinda comes down and we are discovered."

The young ladies dashed to the side of the room and put away their blades. They quickly stripped off their gloves and plastrons. Hurrying past Alexander, Miss Rochelle stopped for a brief moment, her lovely face contrite. "I do apologize for our treatment of you last night, but Aunt thought—" She stopped and seemed to have difficulty putting into words what was thought.

Alex gave a soft chuckle. "Thought me an adventurer or, worse, a gamester who has come to inflict more damage on this estate. You needn't look so stricken, Miss Rochelle. Others have voiced similar opinions much of my life. My father chose his own path, and his family never forgave him for his choice. I am well aware what the world thinks of a man who lives life by his wits. But don't be so quick to judge. I would only ask you to remember I am a man of honor and will do what I think best for the estate and for you all."

Elaina, who'd been listening, pulled on her cousin's arm. "Come, we must hurry."

The two young ladies left Alexander alone in the ballroom. He'd seen little to think he'd changed his cousin's mind, but Miss Rochelle seemed to take what he said to heart. His thoughts settled on that young lady. There seemed to be more to her than he'd first thought. No doubt much of her earlier timidity had been forced by the dowager.

At present, he had too much to worry over to be

thinking about his aunt's lovely poor relation. He had no objection to housing and feeding the girl and her brother, and when his aunt removed to the dower house, they would, too. But that wouldn't happen for months.

It was early days yet, and he hoped he could come to some form of intimacy with his newly met family as time went on. Time and patience were the keys. Then he chuckled. It was certain they couldn't be any less welcoming than they'd been. Perhaps things would become more comfortable once they came to see the positive changes he made in their lives.

Sighing, he made his way upstairs to change from his riding clothes. It would never do to wear all his dirt into one of the drawing rooms, for then his aunt would never accept him as a proper gentleman and lord of the manor.

"He said *what?*" Lady Landry's eyes narrowed and her cheeks flushed pink with indignation as she stared at her daughter some thirty minutes later in the small breakfast parlor.

Elaina picked up her coffee cup. "Well, the gist of what he said was that he had myriad foolish ways to find funds to run the estate. All rather distasteful, but the most horrid option he mentioned was to sell the remaining furniture in the drawing rooms."

Valara glared at her cousin for repeating the conversation, then hurriedly turned to the dowager. "Aunt Belinda, he was merely teasing Ellie, and lucky she was he didn't give her a proper set down for her rudeness. We have no right to question in what manner he will run this estate."

The dowager's mouth puckered into a sour pout after she finished the last bit of her toast. "But Elaina was right to question him. He may make promises until the sun sets, but where are the funds to make good on them?"

With a sigh, Valara moved the buttered eggs about on her plate as she held her tongue. It would never do to inform her aunt that everyone held secrets deep in their hearts and no doubt Lord Landry had his. For all they knew, he may have plundered half of Spain during his years at war and had more than enough funds to repair the Chase. Such an ill-gotten fortune certainly wouldn't be something a gentleman would want known, even by his relatives.

After taking another sip, Elaina put her cup down, a thoughtful expression on her face. "I don't know why, Mama, but I believe he is as good as his word. He didn't have to offer to fully restaff the house. He may yet do wonderful things for the estate."

The dowager pushed back from the table and glared at her daughter as if she'd just announced she intended to marry the local baker. "Addington men can be quite charming when it suits their purpose. He wants our acceptance. To be fully acknowledged by his proper family would make up for the years of being ostracized. Don't be fooled by his looks and glib tongue. It is only a matter of time before he loses at the tables or on the racetrack, and all his good intentions will fly."

That possibility existed, but Valara shook her head in disagreement. "I think we are allowing Uncle Bart's prejudice against his brother to color our opinion of Hugh's son." She straightened her shoulders, for she knew she was about to bring her aunt's wrath down upon her. "I think you should welcome any improvements he might make to the estate and stop treating him like some encroaching mushroom. He is an Addington, after all."

Lady Landry threw her napkin upon the table as she

rose. "He hasn't the least notion of how to carry on as master of a huge estate. Landry Chase is merely a means to supply him with money for his excesses. For every pound he puts in, he will try to take three back. You girls are naive in the ways of the world. Now I must go and speak to Cook about dinner." The baroness marched from the breakfast parlor without a backward glance.

The young ladies exchanged defeated looks across the breakfast table. Valara bit at her lip a moment, then suggested, "We must convince her she will only do more harm with her attitude of distrust and hostility, Ellie."

The younger girl shrugged. "When has Mama ever listened to one of us?" Seeing no point in discussing the matter, Elaina rose. "I am going for a ride before Mama decides to use the horses for some errand to Cley. Will you join me?"

Valara shook her head. "I cannot. I promised the vicar I would sew new shirts for the twins who arrived at the orphanage on Monday. I want to have them finished before I go to give lessons."

Elaina blushed. "You make me ashamed to be thinking of riding when you are doing such good works."

"But, Cousin, I feel certain the twins would be happier if you spent your time galloping about in the meadows than to have their sleeves fall off the first time they donned their shirts." Valara grinned.

With that, Miss Addington picked up her napkin and tossed it playfully at her cousin. "Must you remind me that I have never been able to sew a straight line of stitches?"

Valara rose and came round to her cousin. "And I could never manage a six-foot gate on horseback as you do. We all have our various talents, Ellie. Do not worry your head over the shirts. I am nearly finished. Come, I will help you don your habit until we once again have the luxury of a maid."

A thoughtful expression settled on Elaina's countenance. "Do you think my cousin might buy some new cattle? The carriage horses are such sluggards I am embarrassed to be seen on either of their backs."

"I wouldn't be the least surprised if he did, especially once he sees Polly and Pluto. There is no more mismatched pair in the parish."

As the young ladies envisioned the large chestnut mare and the small dappled gelding Lady Landry was forced to use to pull the carriage, they burst into peals of laughter. The lighthearted moment was soothing to their souls.

In far better spirits, they made their way out of the breakfast parlor, each a little more hopeful things might not be so bad under the new baron's rule.

Lady Landry stopped at the head of the stairs leading to the basement kitchen. Her thoughts dwelled on her niece's assumption that Bartholomew was the reason for her dislike of her husband's youngest brother. Ironically, Hugh had been the first Addington man she'd met. He'd been so handsome coming across the ballroom floor to ask her, Belinda Milford, to dance so many years ago. She hadn't cared a fig that he was third in line to a barony. She would have given him her heart at that moment.

A wave of bitterness rose in her throat. But he hadn't wanted her or her heart, had he? He'd danced with her, flirted a little, introduced her to Lord Landry—a thinner, paler version of the glorious Hugh—he then moved on to the other girls making their come out that Season, dancing with and teasing them just as he had her. She was completely bowled over on that first meeting.

Yet despite her outrageous flirting with Bart over the course of the following weeks, Hugh paid little attention. All her coquetting had gotten her was her father's demand that she accept Lord Landry's offer, which came unexpectedly within a fortnight of their meeting. She'd been so intent on capturing true love that she'd quite forgotten her father would demand the gentleman with a title and estates. Her marriage had been a misery, and Belinda knew who was to blame: Hugh Addington and his indifference.

The dowager tugged her fichu into position on her shoulders, her mouth pursed into a grimace, making her look more embittered than thoughtful. She couldn't exact her revenge on a dead man, but she could certainly make his son pay. Her mouth relaxed into a satisfied grin and she plodded down the stairs. Her mind teamed with plots and plans to drive the new young lord from the Chase as soon as may be. She was halfway down the worn stone steps before she realized voices echoed up the narrow stairway from the kitchen. She stopped to listen, and her eyes widened as recognition dawned. For some outlandish reason, her nephew was conferring with Cook. Whatever could he be about?

Curious, she began to steal slowly down the remaining steps to eavesdrop on the conversation. Perhaps she would be able to hinder whatever plans he might make.

In the roomy kitchen below, Alexander stood facing Cook, or rather the woman who'd been enacting that role since the Chase's real cook could no longer tolerate the family's straitened circumstances and had departed. Mrs. Brock, a stout woman in her late sixties with gray curls hanging from her starched bonnet, was full of apologies for the meal of the previous evening.

"It weren't my best efforts, my lord. But Lady Landry insisted it must be the plainest of English fare."

"To be sure, Mrs. Brock. I have not come to discuss last night's dinner. As I said, I am offering those servants who have been with the family for years the opportunity to be pensioned off with a good annuity. It is clear to me many of you are still here long past your time simply because the late baron couldn't or wouldn't provide you with a proper stipend."

"Yer offering to pension us off properlike, my lord?" There was a hopeful look in the old woman's faded brown eyes.

"I am. In return, I hope you are willing to stay until Bainbridge finds people to fill your—"

Suddenly a shriek filled the kitchen, followed by a loud thumping sound. At the far end of the room, a large bundle of black bombazine, white petticoats, and flailing arms and legs crashed onto the landing of the stairs, then tumbled down the three steps that angled to the kitchen floor. With a loud groan, the strange ball untangled into the unconscious form of Lady Landry, her cap lost on the stairs, her fichu hanging backward under her double chin like a child's bib.

Cook's hands flew to her face as she gasped, "Her ladyship's done tumbled down the stairs. Saints preserve us, she's dead."

Alexander crossed the slate floor to his aunt. He knelt to test her limbs, but could find no broken bones, and her breathing held steady despite a rapidly growing lump on her forehead. "Not dead, Mrs. Brock. Knocked unconscious."

The patter of running feet echoed on the stone steps. Within minutes, Valara Rochelle, Elaina Addington, and the old footman, Jonas, appeared at the landing. Elaina's eyes widened at the sight of her mother prostrate on the floor.

She rushed down the remaining stairs, Valara right behind her, and pushed his lordship aside. The ladies knelt beside the fallen dowager. Elaina glared up at Alexander. "What have you done to Mama?"

Mrs. Brock chided, "Now, Miss Elaina, what can ye

be thinkin'? Lord Landry was here talkin' with me when yer mama took a tumble down them stairs."

Elaina had the decency to blush, but she offered no apology. Instead she turned her attention to her mother, trying to waken her by patting her cheek as Valara held the lady's hand and called to her aunt.

Valara looked up, her blue eyes filled with concern. "My lord, I think we must send someone for the doctor."

Alex nodded grimly. "Perhaps your brother will go, for I shall need Jonas here to help carry her ladyship to her rooms."

The young lady's cheeks flamed. "I am sorry, my lord, but Neville is rarely out of bed before noon. It would take him thirty minutes to be ready. It really should be someone who might leave anon."

A frown wrinkled Alexander's brow. He would need to find something to occupy the boy if he had nothing better to do than sleep away the better part of the day. It seemed strange that the lad could be keeping late hours, for he understood that the family rarely went out and last night they'd all retired by ten.

"I shall go," a voice echoed in the cavernous kitchen.

Everyone looked up to see Sir Roger standing on the landing, concern etched on his face as his gaze locked with Elaina Addington's. He'd changed from his riding clothes and was dressed in a nut brown coat with a soft yellow waistcoat over tan pantaloons, his blond hair neatly combed about his handsome face.

"An excellent suggestion. Miss Rochelle, pray give Sir Roger directions."

Valara rose. "It is quite simple, sir. Once you leave the front gate, follow the road west. Dr. Macy's house is the second past the tower mill, which you cannot miss."

Elaina, who hadn't taken her gaze off the baronet

since he'd first spoken, seemed to come out of her daze. "Pray hurry, sir."

Nodding, the baronet disappeared back up the stairs, the sound of his rapid footsteps soon fading. Elaina returned her attention to her mother. "We must take her to her rooms at once. This cold floor is doing her no good."

"I quite agree, Cousin." Alexander, not unaccustomed to dealing with injuries, determined they would have need of two grooms, if there were still that many employed, as well as Jonas. The footman went to summon the men. Alexander tried to reassure the young ladies the dowager would be fine, but knew his words held little value to them.

The footman returned in a matter of minutes with a burly groom he called Henry and an ancient gardener who tugged off his felt cap to announce he was Tom. After a great deal of effort on the part of the four strong men, the lady was at last safely settled in bed, her daughter and niece in attendance while they awaited the doctor.

About to retreat to the library to await the doctor's arrival, Alexander drew Miss Rochelle aside. "I shall leave you ladies to the task of making the dowager comfortable, but do come and inform me of the doctor's prognosis. Please know if there is anything my aunt needs, I shall do my best to procure it."

The young lady, never taking her eyes from the lady on the bed, distractedly said, "You are very kind, and I shall come directly to you on hearing what must be done." With that, she closed the bedchamber door.

He stood gazing at the door, thinking Miss Rochelle was quite the prettiest lady he'd ever seen. Then he shook himself out of his stupor, realizing that he had business matters awaiting his attention. He didn't fool himself about the reason the lady had been less hostile

than the others. Her situation here at the Chase, as well
as the boy's, depended very much on his benevolence.
As he made his way to the library, he wondered if this
family crisis might signal a new beginning for the family.
Difficulties surmounted as a group often brought people
together, or so he hoped. It would certainly make life
much more pleasant at the Chase if they could all be
civil.

On entering the library, Alexander went to his desk
and got to work. He knew one surefire way to make
peace with the dowager was to return the estate to its
former profitable self.

Some thirty minutes later, Alexander looked up from
the list he'd penned of the number and variety of livestock needing to be purchased for the estate when a
loud knocking at the front door echoed in the front
hall. Thinking the doctor had at last arrived, the baron
rose and entered the hall, intent on introducing himself
to the medical man, since they would, no doubt, be
seeing one another from time to time in the small society of a country village.

But to Alex's surprise, when Jonas opened the door,
the visitor proved to be a man in a blue and white uniform, the style of which was unknown to the baron. The
soldier, if that was what he was, was tall and powerfully
built, with a smattering of freckles on his face. His red
hair had been neatly combed, but still sprang in unruly
curls from under his black hat.

"Captain Waite to see Lord Landry at once, my good
fellow," the gentleman snapped at the footman, as if
he were addressing a raw recruit.

Stepping forward, Alexander gave a brief nod of his
head. "I am Landry."

"My lord, might I have a moment of your time? There

is a matter of some import of which I wish to speak."
The officer's tone grew only slightly more defferential
as he stepped into the hall and surrendered his hat to
the footman.

Alexander politely ushered the man into his library.
Once settled behind his desk, he inquired, "What
brings you to Landry Chase, Captain?"

The gentleman stood ramrod stiff, having refused a
seat. "My lord, I am currently assigned to the Customs
House in Cley. It's my job to curb the smuggling in
these parts."

"A thankless job, no doubt." Alexander smiled at the
man, but got only a hostile stare in return.

After a moment, Waite said, "Quite so, my lord. Is it
true you were with Wellington in the Peninsula and at
Waterloo?"

"I was with the duke for many years." Alexander was
surprised at the wistful sound in his voice. "But that
seems a lifetime ago as I face the difficulties of managing an estate."

The captain nodded and seemed to relax a bit. "Then
you'll understand, my lord, I'm only doing my duty. Last
night there was a landing nearby. Unfortunately, we
were too late to catch them, but after they scattered we
followed several of the rascals."

Alexander listened with mild interest. Waite was telling him nothing he hadn't surmised about this part of
Norfolk. In truth, when one lived on the coast in any
country, one could scarcely avoid free-traders. He'd
even noted the sliver of a moon the night before produced almost no light. "Are you telling me smugglers
are in the habit of using my estate to land their illegal
cargo?"

"Aye, my lord, they are. And there is worse yet. We
stumbled across one of their trails and it led us straight
to the manor. The culprit was able to stay just ahead of

us before we lost him in the woods, but we are almost certain he came here."

Alexander sat up straight. "The person came to the Chase, Captain?" The movement Sir Roger had seen the previous night leaped into Alex's mind.

The man nodded. "We've suspected someone in this house has been involved with the free-traders for some time."

A slow, burning anger began to build within Alexander. Someone in the Chase had been skulking about in the darkness last night helping common smugglers. Sir Roger hadn't imagined what he'd seen at the window. But who?

Then it hit Alexander with the force of a hammer. Neville Rochelle! His nocturnal activities would account for his still being abed so late in the day. Besides, who else but a young boy would foolishly engage in a lark to liven his dreary existence—or, worse yet, do it to line his pockets? Either way, Alex intended to put a stop to it at once.

Realizing that the Riding Officer was watching him, Alexander sank back in the chair. "You can be certain, Captain, that I was unaware any illegal activities were occurring. I shall not tolerate such conduct. I assure you, if someone in this house has engaged in smuggling it will happen no more."

Waite's eyes narrowed as he locked his thumbs into the leather belt that bound his uniform. "Well, my lord, I was hoping to question—"

Alexander rose, his face a haughty mask. He effectively put an end to what the man had been about to say as he stared down his nose at him. There could be no thought of surrendering a foolish schoolboy who'd involved himself in something far more serious than he'd realized. Miss Rochelle would never forgive him if he allowed the revenue officer to question her brother, though why that mattered was beyond him at the moment. "As I said, if a member of this household was involved, it is now at an end." His tone brooked no argument.

There was little doubt that the young officer was not well pleased as he glared at the baron, but even he could not gainsay a peer. "Very good, my lord." He turned and went to the door, then stopped as he placed his hand on the handle. Looking back over his shoulder, he defiantly added, "But be warned, there shall be no special treatment if we catch someone with the goods."

"I would expect none, Captain. Good day." Alexander nodded a dismissal.

The baron stood frozen like a statue for several moments after the library door shut. His first thought was to charge upstairs and drag that young cawker out of bed by the scruff of his nightshirt and give him a rare trimming, as he would have done with any man in his regiment who violated the law. But his experience in dealing with young men had taught him to master his own anger before he confronted their excuses.

With that in mind, he went to the door and summoned Jonas. "Please wake Mr. Rochelle. I will see him in the library in fifteen minutes. No excuses."

"Very good, my lord." The old man hurried up the stairs.

After closing the door, Alexander settled down to ponder what he would say to this young man he scarcely knew. There was no blood tie to either Neville or his sister, but Alex knew he'd inherited them, along with his duty to Lady Landry and her daughter. He would make the boy understand that as long as he resided at the Chase, Alex would expect him to abide by his rules.

Four

A rather disheveled young man appeared in the library in the time allotted. Alexander noted that Neville Rochelle looked more an eager puppy than a free-trader. The boy's pale brown curls poked out in tufts in all directions. His ill-cut garments appeared too large for his slender frame, several buttons were undone on his waistcoat, and his hastily tied cravat hung askew.

After several bleary-eyed blinks, Neville inquired, "You wished to see me, my lord?"

Much of Alex's anger fled in a flash of insight. If the boy were involved in smuggling, it could only be for a foolish lark. Too often boredom led young men into mischief. He'd seen it with the young recruits in his brigade during the long winter lapses between battles. One could surmise Mr. Rochelle had received no male guidance from Bartholomew Addington. But perhaps that wasn't such a bad thing, considering their uncle's propensity for dissipation.

The baron rose from the desk and moved toward two brown leather armchairs before the fire. He gestured to the other seat. "Do you often sleep past noon, Mr. Rochelle?"

The young man blushed, but gamely settled into the chair his lordship had offered. "I have often suffered from an inability to sleep, my lord. It helps if I read until the wee hours of the morning. Is there some problem?"

Alexander settled down and eyed the boy thoughtfully before saying, "I hope not, but that is a matter I would like to discuss with you. Before we begin, however, I wish you to understand that with the death of your uncle Bart, I feel the responsibility for you and your sister, though you are not related to me, has fallen to my shoulders. I am a stranger to you at present, but I hope with time you can come to think of me as you did your uncle."

A look of horror settled on Mr. Rochelle's rather delicate face. "I certainly hope that shall never happen."

Alex's mouth arched downward. They all were determined to hate him, it seemed. "Mr. Rochelle, contrary to what your aunt chooses to think, I am not the devil incarnate. I intend—"

The young man threw back his head and laughed. "You misunderstand me, my lord. I hope I shall never think of you as I did Uncle Bart. The man was a complete and utter rotter. I disliked him intensely, as did most people who crossed his path. I would guess he earned himself a seat closest to the fire in Hades." Neville sobered, and then with dignity added, "I would be honored to have you act the role of my guardian, my lord, even if there is no legal formality."

Folding his hands in front of him, Alexander wondered how long that would last once a set of rules was put into force. Yet he suspected the boy would not chafe so much if he had someone to take an interest in him. "Excellent! The first thing I would recommend is that we dispense with our strained formality and behave as most families do. My friends call me Alexander."

"And I am Neville." The young man leaned across the space between the two chairs and shook the baron's hand.

The two men surveyed one another in wary silence a moment, neither quite sure what to expect from the other. At last Alexander said, "I fear I have a rather prickly subject on which I must begin our new relationship. I had a visit this morning from Captain Waite. Do you know the gentleman, Neville?"

The boy snorted and his face changed into a mask of disdain. "Everybody knows the Riding Officer. Cley is a small village, and that fool Waite has accused most everyone in the parish from the vicar to the magistrate of being in league with the smugglers at one time or another."

Alex stored that bit of information for future use. In truth, the captain might not be that far off the mark. Too often people looked the other way when the crime didn't involve them directly or when they could buy French brandy well below price. Still, Alex didn't want Neville to misunderstand his views on the matter of being involved. Most people considered smuggling a victimless crime and therefore not so bad, but as a former soldier, Alex knew the revenues the Customs Board collected were important in financing the military.

"Remember, my boy, a fool he may be, but he has dragoons stationed nearby who can and will use deadly force to uphold the law of the land."

As only the young can, the boy's expression shifted to one of airy unconcern. "There's never been a smuggler shot in these parts since I've lived here."

"There is always a first time, and I shouldn't like that person to be a member of this family."

Neville's pale blue eyes widened. "What are you saying, sir?"

Alexander slid forward on his seat. "Waite followed someone to this house last night. I don't want to have to be the one to tell your sister you were shot dead on the marsh some dark night."

The young man's cheeks grew ashen. "I swear to you, Alexander, I am not involved with the free-traders. I would never risk our situation at the Chase in such a foolish manner. My aunt sets great store by appearances, and she would surely put us from the house for embarrassing her in such a manner. I—"

The door to the library flew open, startling both men. Miss Rochelle hurried into the room, the color in her cheeks heightened, whether from anger or concern Alex didn't know.

"Jonas tells me that you demanded to see my brother, Lord Landry. Is there some problem?"

Her anxious expression made her look too vulnerable for Alexander's peace of mind. He rose and gestured her to take his seat, but she shook her head.

Hoping to convince her nothing terrible was happening to Neville, he casually asked, "How is my aunt?"

"The doctor is with her now." The young lady moved to stand beside her brother. "What is this matter that demanded my brother's sleep be disturbed?"

Neville took his sister's hand. The concern the boy felt for her was reflected in his eyes and reminded the baron of his own sisters. Brothers instinctively tried to protect their siblings.

"Don't worry, Lara. 'Tis a mere misunderstanding. I can handle things. Go back upstairs and help Elaina."

The young lady shook her head. "I want to hear the worst, Nev."

Hoping to put an end to the lady's fears, Alexander said, "Miss Rochelle, your brother and I were just discussing Captain Waite and the smuggling here in Norfolk. The officer and his men trailed someone to the Chase last night."

Neville shrugged, giving a half grin. "He thinks it was me."

The lady's cheeks grew a deep pink, and her eyes

darkened with anger. "How dare you accuse my brother without the least proof? It could be anyone at the Chase—or no one, for that matter. Perhaps it was someone passing close by the manor house in an effort to elude Waite and his men."

Tapping his fingers thoughtfully on the mantelpiece, the baron nodded. "That is a possibility. Still, try to look at things from my perspective. I must know if I harbor a smuggler. And of the people in the house, your brother's youth and innocence make him the most likely candidate for such a foolish escapade. Everyone else is either female or old." Having made his point, Alexander crossed his arms and stared at the outraged beauty.

Valara Rochelle straightened, her chin held high. "My lord, if you believe Neville is capable of involving himself in such lawlessness for mere money, my brother and I can leave Landry Chase this very afternoon."

Despite her bold announcement, Alexander could see fear in her blue eyes. Clearly, she was terrified he might take her at her word. They had nowhere to go, and even if he had learned Neville was involved, Alex would never be so cruel as to force them out of the Chase.

"Miss Rochelle, there is no need for such drastic action. Neville swears he is no free-trader, and I am inclined to believe him. I hope you will stay. I know your cousin and aunt would miss you both. Bainbridge tells me you fulfilled many of my aunt's duties when there were still tenants. I shall certainly need similar assistance once the cottages are repaired and filled with families."

The brother and sister glanced at one another in relief. Neville patted her hand and the stiffness seemed to flow from her as she slumped against the boy. "Lara, I think there is a great deal we can both do to help Alexander put right what Uncle Bart ruined."

She nodded, then looked at the baron. "Very well, sir. We shall stay and do our part to help you."

"Then the first thing you must do is feed your brother. I fear I roused him from his slumbers rather abruptly to answer my questions. Neville, would you care to join me for a ride this afternoon? I need someone to show me the Chase's windmill that Mr. Bailey tells me I must inspect. The two Arabians I purchased in London were delivered early this morning, and I should like to test their wind a bit."

The prospect of new horse flesh in the stables made Neville's blue eyes twinkle. "New prads! I should love to go, Alexander."

"And would you care to join us, Miss Rochelle? I can borrow a mount from Sir Roger if you don't wish to ride one of Lady Landry's horses."

She smiled but shook her head. "I prefer to walk most places, my lord. Elaina is the horsewoman of the family."

"Don't let her fool you, sir. She has a very good seat, but it's her blue habit. It hasn't fit properly since she grew so tall." Neville took no note of his sister's marked blush. Instead, his thoughts were concentrated on his stomach. "Come, Lara, I am famished."

The young man made for the door, but Miss Rochelle held back. She nervously fidgeted with the buttons on her black gown. "I do apologize for losing my temper, but I have always taken care of my brother, and I fear I am a bit overprotective."

Alexander leaned against the mantelpiece and smiled. "Miss Rochelle, I have two sisters myself. I know what they can be like when roused to the defense of a loved one. I took no offense."

She gave a warm smile, then turned and joined her brother, who awaited her at the door.

As the pair departed, Alexander realized the more he

saw of her, the more he liked Valara Rochelle. Her fierce defense of her brother showed a great deal of courage and spirit, especially considering that he could have taken her up on her offer for them to leave. He was surprised that she was still on the shelf, but perhaps few had seen her in Society. He didn't know how his aunt treated her in public: as a beloved niece, or a poor relation? People often took their cues from such treatment.

He suddenly was struck with a thought that would improve everyone's situation here at the Chase, something that might garner the approval of even his aunt. He strode to his desk and pulled out paper and pen. He would write to Lady Margaret. She would know just what he wanted. With that, he dipped the pen in the inkstand and began to write.

Mrs. Brock placed a full plate in front of Neville. "Here's a treat for ye, my boy." Upon bobbing a curtsy, Cook ambled from the breakfast parlor.

He looked across the table at his sister, surprised delight etched on his face. "Beefsteak! We haven't had that since Uncle Bart gamed away the last of the shorthorns." Without waiting for his sister to comment, he picked up his knife and fork, going to work on his breakfast in earnest.

"Mrs. Brock tells me his lordship has the steward settling all the estate's accounts in Cley. The butcher was first and delivered fresh meat immediately." Valara poured herself a cup of coffee and allowed her brother to enjoy his breakfast, an indulgent smile on her face as he moaned pleasurably with each bite of the long denied treat. While she should be upstairs with her cousin awaiting the doctor's verdict about her aunt, she had an important question she wanted to put to her brother.

Neville, savoring every morsel, held up a speared piece of beefsteak and gazed at it thoughtfully for several minutes before he announced, "I don't care what Aunt Belinda says, Alexander is a great gun." With that he devoured the slice.

Valara was beginning to feel the same, but she hadn't been raked over the coals by the baron that morning. "You don't mind that he accused you of being a smuggler?"

"I can see where someone could jump to the wrong conclusion. I am the only man about other than a bunch of ancient servants. I have to admit it was a bit of a facer, but I could see his point once he explained." The young man cut off another slice of meat, being surprisingly understanding after the fact.

Valara fingered the handle of her cup a moment before she put the question to him. "You haven't ever been out on the marshes at night, have you?"

A swift shadow of what she would swear was guilt flashed across her brother's face, but it was gone in an instant, replaced with indignation.

"You heard me swear I was not involved with smugglers, yet you question my truthfulness?"

"Oh, Nev, don't be angry. Someone was obviously near the Chase last night and likely stole into this house. I thought perhaps you denied any involvement to protect our situation here. I won't be upset if you will only tell me the truth. I know you have been very bored and lonely, especially since most of your old friends have gone to Oxford."

Neville carefully avoided looking directly at her. Instead he stared at a moth-eaten tapestry hanging behind her that had escaped his uncle's clutches due to its sad state. "My word was enough for his lordship, who is nearly a stranger, and I should hope it is enough for my own sister." With that he rose and stormed from the room, the picture of wounded dignity.

Valara's first instinct was to go after him and apologize, but there was something unsettling in his manner that caused her to fear the worst. Had he involved himself with the Gentlemen? The very thought made a shiver go up her spine, knowing what she did about smugglers.

She'd been scarcely fifteen the first summer of their arrival in Norfolk, and she had been utterly enchanted by the beautiful, remote dunes and flat salt marshes—that is, until she'd overheard a conversation between the butler and one of the former footmen about a body that had washed ashore near Cromer. Work of the free-traders, had been the men's conclusion, retribution for a man having been seen talking with the Riding Officer. Smugglers were a rough and dangerous lot.

More frightening still was Captain Waite's determination to bring the gentlemen to justice. He'd been at Cley's Customs House for nearly a year with nothing to show for his efforts, and the passing time seemed only to make him more vigilant. He positively haunted the marshes with his men on moonless nights. She couldn't bear to think about her only brother in the gaol at Holt or lost to her by a dragoon's bullet.

Her cooler self soon took control, and she realized there was still a possibility someone else at the Chase might be involved. After all, the cellars had always been full of brandy when nothing else had been in abundant supply. Yet somehow she couldn't envision either Bainbridge or Jonas traipsing about the marshes in the dark. That brought her straight back to her brother. For the first time in the nine years since they'd lived at the Chase, Lara was truly afraid for Neville. She must do something to protect him from the lure of such adventure, but what?

Uncertain why, she had an urge to go to Lord Landry and confess her fears, but what would he do if he found Neville had lied? He'd shown a pronounced distaste for the Gentlemen and the idea that someone at the Chase might be involved, but there had been such kindness in his eyes when he'd accepted her apology. She thought she might trust him. Still, she hesitated, realizing she scarcely knew the man and shouldn't foolishly risk the roof over their head on a whim. Besides, she didn't know for certain Neville was involved.

If only he had more to occupy his restless spirit. He needed a masculine influence, a steadying hand. Then it struck her. She must send a message to Uncle Philippe. Neville was his heir, and the man had it within his power to remove the boy from Landry Chase to save him from his foolish pranks. She'd done all the *comte* had asked her to do when last he visited. Surely he would come when he knew Neville might face danger. Convinced her uncle was the only solution, she rose and hurried to her room to pen the letter.

Dr. Macy departed from the Chase some thirty minutes after Alexander's conversation with the Rochelles. He spoke briefly with the baron, informing him Lady Landry's injuries, while not extremely serious, would require several weeks to heal. Both her ankle and knee were badly wrenched, and she had suffered a serious bump on the head. After refusing a glass of brandy, the doctor left, but not before giving his lordship a sincere welcome to the Chase.

As to his aunt's condition, Alexander couldn't deny being deprived of the lady's company for a fortnight would be no hardship. She appeared to be an unhappy woman who spread her wrath equally among her relations and the staff, but especially to Alex and Sir Roger.

With both his cousin and Miss Rochelle keeping vigil in the sickroom, Alexander ran Sir Roger to ground in the manor's main salon, where he'd settled after returning with the doctor. Sir Roger sat before a small fire in a paint-chipped gilt chair—one of the few remaining in the room—sipping a glass of brandy, a thoughtful expression on his face.

Alexander found an equally battered chair and turned it backward to straddle it, propping his arms on the back. "It's been quite a morning."

"You owe me three pounds." Sir Roger grinned as his friend sat down.

"I owe you a great deal more than that for putting up with all you've faced here. But what caused you to spend money on my behalf?"

"The sum was owed to the doctor for past services. His wife refused to give me his direction until the debt was cleared." The baronet looked back at the fire. "It seems Lady Landry is not a favorite with Mrs. Macy. I come to think you will be greatly admired by the locals once they realize you shall be putting money back in their pockets."

Alexander sighed, thinking once again about his uncle's maltreatment not only of the estate but the local citizens. It made his aunt's dislike of him all the more puzzling. Putting her from his mind for the moment, he turned the discussion to the day's other unexpected event. He explained about the Riding Officer's visit and the results of his interview with young Neville.

"Do you think you can trust the boy's word?" Sir Roger's question echoed in the empty room.

"I have decided to find out this evening." Alexander stared into the flames of the dying fire, his amber eyes holding a determined glint.

"Will you stand watch?" Sir Roger turned a curious eye on his friend.

"I shall. There should be little or no moon this evening. One can be certain the Gentlemen will be about their business somewhere along this coast tonight. Whoever is involved at the Chase will, no doubt, have tasks to fulfill, and I shall be there to put an end to our resident smuggler once and for all."

"Hopefully you don't mean to exclude me from the adventure." Sir Roger straightened as if he meant to dash headlong into the woods to stand guard at that very moment.

Alexander nodded his head. "I hoped you would lend me your support, since I cannot watch all sides of this building at once."

"I should like nothing better than a little excitement."

A case clock in the hall chimed the hour. Alexander rose from the chair. "Neville is taking me to inspect the Chase's windmill. The steward wants me to give approval for some rather major repairs so the place can be put back into operation as soon as may be. Care to join us?"

Sir Roger's gaze went back to the fire and he shook his head. "I shall remain here in case Miss Addington—er, the ladies should have need of something."

Alexander gazed thoughtfully at his friend, saying nothing about the baronet's decided interest in Elaina. He didn't need to tell his friend his suit certainly would not be welcomed by Lady Landry.

After changing into riding clothes, Alexander strolled down to the stables, where an excited Neville awaited him. The two Arabians were saddled and ready, their chestnut coats shining like burnished copper in the afternoon sun. The boy chattered like a magpie about the horses' fine points even as they mounted and trotted down the gravel drive. After some minutes, the animal's qualities had been exhausted, and Alexander got an opportunity to change the subject.

"Tell me, Neville, how do you amuse yourself here in Norfolk?"

The animated expression dropped from the boy's face. "There is little enough to do. Lara insists that I take lessons with the vicar who runs the orphanage. She says a future *comte* cannot be illiterate, though why it should matter, I cannot think. My uncle Philippe has neither estates nor fortune for me to inherit in France. I shall likely have to make my way in the navy or some other profession."

Knowing almost nothing of the Rochelles' circumstances, Alexander asked the boy several questions about his French uncle, but Neville knew very little save that the man was back in France trying to improve his situation. "Lara knows more than I about the family. You must speak with her for such details."

Alexander decided that would be no hardship. "So you are working at being a scholar. What about your sister and my cousin? Before their mourning, did they have suitors?" Strangely, he was anxious to know the answer, but he decided it was because it was his duty to see the young ladies properly settled.

Neville guided his horse through a gate in the stone fence and closed the gate before he answered the baron's question. "Elaina and the Earl of Westoke have been expected to make a match for years, not that the gentleman has shown the least inclination to visit my cousin since she and Lady Blythe were foolish enough to don men's apparel and ride to the hunt some years back. He's never forgiven Ellie for having interrupted a party he was attending with the Prince Regent. He had to return because his sister broke an arm trying to take a fence." The young man grew quiet a moment, then added, "Ellie should have known better than to involve Bly. She's a game little thing but ain't up to all my cousin's rigs."

Alexander suddenly wondered if Elaina Addington were a complete hoyden, but he let the matter drop for the present. "Your family and the earl's were close?"

"Until the accident and the death of Lady Westoke. Ellie and Bly—Lady Blythe, that is—grew up here together, but Westoke shipped her off to school after she recovered. Said we were a bad influence. Aunt Belinda blamed Lara for not having stopped them from going, but they hadn't told either one of us what they intended." There was a hint of wounded pride in the boy's voice, as if he were still angry at being excluded from the escapade despite the outcome.

"So my cousin is destined for Lord Westoke, should he deign to forgive her. What of your sister?" Alex tried to keep his voice from sounding too interested.

"My guess is Lara will end up marrying someone like the vicar, since she spends much of her time working at the orphanage when not helping Aunt Belinda. Of course, I would far rather she wed Mr. Akers than the Reverend Mr. Binion. Old Binny's a bit of a prosy fellow."

"Akers?" Alex knew a sudden dislike for the unknown man who had garnered Neville's approval for his sister's hand.

"Mr. Ronald Akers. Owns a small estate on the edge of the Chase." Neville pointed off in the direction where the road they'd just left continued toward Cromer. "A very friendly chap. Aunt Belinda thinks him a mushroom because he don't hunt, but that's because he ain't fond of horses. He does like sailing and, of all things, racing birds. Claims a pigeon can be trained to fly straight back to its home dovecote in a matter of hours without losing its way. I find all his talk of birds a dead bore, but before Uncle Bart died, Akers often took us out on his small sloop. That was great fun."

Just then the two men rounded a stand of trees and the windmill came into view across the flat meadow, chasing all else from Alexander's mind. It was an impressive structure, standing some four stories high on the edge of the salt marsh, the choppy dark water of the North Sea in constant motion behind the round tower. The drab gray flintstone building had a single line of windows, one some five feet atop the other, all the way to the white-capped top. Four white wooden spars, looking as if they hadn't been painted in years, radiated out from the cap to a length of some twenty feet. Yet despite the steady breeze off the sea, the mill's arms stood motionless, the canvas sails furled in disuse.

As they drew closer, a small squat building could be seen standing to one side of the mill, which Neville explained was where the miller would live when one was employed.

"The place looks rather old." Alexander scanned the tower and adjoining building, deciding both seemed to be in reasonably good state despite their age.

"I believe it was constructed by the first baron at the same time as the Chase. Bailey says it could last another hundred years if it's put back in operation. The main shaft that drives the mill splintered two years ago during a storm. The miller never explained why all the sails hadn't been properly furled during the tempest, but he had a fondness for ale. Truth be told, it cost him his position, since Uncle Bart swore there was no money to order a new shaft. But most of the tenants were leaving, as well, so there was little grain to be milled. Now it just sits here."

The men tied their horses to a rail, then entered the windmill. The main room was surprisingly clean of flour; the large grinding wheel and cogs looked in good condition despite the recent disuse.

Neville motioned to his lordship. "Come, I shall show you where the break in the shaft is and the view from the top." He hurried up a set of stairs that lined the far wall, and Alexander had little choice but to follow. They climbed up three floors before the young man stopped and gestured at the broken shaft. The wood, some six inches in diameter, had disintegrated into thousands of splinters and was a twisted mass. The entire shaft would need to be replaced, since it ran all the way up the middle of the structure, and that would be a large task.

After closely inspecting the break, Alexander allowed Neville to coax him up to the top floor. At the highest window, he stood awed by the stark beauty of the Norfolk coastline. "You can see for miles from here."

He stared down the long expanse of empty shoreline, watching the waves break at the edge of the grassy marsh. The sight was beautiful. Then Alex was struck by a thought. One could see in an instant why the Riding Officer had such a difficult task in this part of England. There wasn't a single house between here and Cley save the abandoned dower house. It would take a veritable army of men to watch this shoreline for smugglers.

The sea and the wind were inadvertently aligned against the Customs men, washing away any evidence that someone might have landed along this isolated stretch of land. The marsh grass waving in the wind only made the beach look more remote. In the distance, the top of Cley's windmill gleamed brightly among the red tile roofs of the houses.

Neville shoved open the window and pointed back to the left. "You can even see the Chase from here."

Alexander leaned out and was surprised to find the chimney pots and slate tiles of the roof of the manor scarcely half a mile from where the mill was situated behind a wide belt of trees. "I had no idea we were so close."

"The first baron planted the woods as a windbreak off the sea. The wind can be frightful during a winter storm. One can walk here from the manor far faster than going by the road, but the paths through the woods are a bit narrow for horses."

Alexander suddenly wondered if the person Captain Waite had discovered last night might have been coming from the windmill. At the time he hadn't known the building was so close to the Chase. Then he realized despite the mill's proximity to the shore, it would be the last place smugglers would store their booty, because no doubt it would be the first place Waite would search when looking for casks of brandy.

Neville chattered on. "Bly, Elaina, Lara, and I used to love coming here to watch the miller work. Old Grubbs would let us sit up here to watch the sun go down. When he was done working, he'd come up and let me help him furl the sails."

To Alexander's surprise, Neville stepped through the window onto a small iron balcony that ringed the top of the windmill. The slender young man reached up and unlashed one of the canvas sails, then pulled it free and hooked it to a wooden pole that extended from the top of the spar. The sail, which narrowed to a point at the bottom of the spar, billowed out and filled with wind. A creaking protest sounded in the depths of the mill as the main shaft tried to turn. Alexander ordered the boy to furl the sail before more damage could be done.

"Oh, it cannot turn with only one of the sails unfurled. Especially not since the shaft broke." But he did as he was told. Within minutes, he had the sail once again wrapped about the long spar.

Watching the boy work, Alexander knew he must put

the great old mill to rights. It was as much a part of Landry Chase's legacy as the land. It would be a shame to allow it to sit unused. He would inform Mr. Bailey to replace the shaft as soon as possible. Also, it wouldn't hurt to have a miller once again on site to keep an eye on the comings and goings along this coast.

Later, as they cantered back to the Chase, Alexander's thoughts returned to the problem of determining if he housed a smuggler. He intended to discover the answer that evening. He had too much to do putting the manor and estate to rights to spend his time worrying about smugglers.

Near four o'clock that afternoon, Bainbridge arrived back from Holt, accompanied by a bevy of servants eager to take up their new positions. After assigning everyone rooms and tasks, the butler came to the library to inform Alexander of his return. The baron complimented the man on his success, then dismissed him in a distracted manner. As the old servant was about to depart, Alexander rose and asked, "Can you tell me the way to the roof, Bainbridge?"

"The roof?" The butler's eyes widened in surprise. "It likely isn't safe, my lord. There are several places where it leaks."

"I should like to see for myself." Alexander waited patiently. He wanted to reconnoiter the best spot to watch for any movement that evening.

The butler, recovering his sangfroid, quickly informed his lordship how to reach the attics which led to the roof. Alex made his way up to the top of the manor. The door to the roof was easy to find, and it opened to a view of the front drive. He stepped out into the fading light and smelled pitch warmed by the day's sun and salt air. The temperature had dropped along with the setting sun. The rising slate roof and chimneys obscured his view of the sea, but he could see the front gate. He stepped to the edge and peered over to see the old gardener, Tom, walking the new men over the grounds. Alexander could only assume he was giving them instructions about where to begin on the morrow.

He made his way around the border of the roof, inspecting the ground below. He could make out several paths that disappeared into the nearby woods. One headed toward the mill, and he would guess that he would find one that led toward Cley once he was on the other side of the manor. Turning the corner, he halted in surprise. A cloaked figure stood on the far corner of the roof facing the sea. A sudden gust of wind tugged at the black velvet material, dragging down the hood and revealing tousled blond curls.

What the devil was Miss Rochelle doing on the roof? Standing quietly observing her, Alex thought she looked terribly lonely with the stormy sea behind her. He was suddenly struck with how well one could see the vista of the water from atop the manor. His gaze locked on the sails of a small sloop making for Cley. The Chase would be perfect for a lookout.

Was it possible Valara Rochelle and her brother were involved in this illegal business? Or was he jumping to conclusions? Somehow he didn't see the lady involving herself, or her brother, in such a perilous enterprise. From what Neville had said, Elaina was more likely to do so than the reserved Miss Rochelle.

There was no point in engaging in idle speculation. He made his way to her without making a sound, not wishing to disturb her.

The lady appeared engrossed by the sight of the distant sea, or was she merely deep in thought? "Miss Rochelle?"

She started when he spoke. She turned, and her

cheeks flamed pink. "My lord, I didn't hear you approach."

"You did seem in rather a brown study. I fear even a penny couldn't purchase such heavy thoughts."

She smiled, then turned to face the sea, the wind pulling the blond tendrils back from her face. "Over the years, I have found this is the best place to sort out my thoughts when things worry me."

He leaned on the parapet, the better to see her lovely face. "May I be of some help with whatever problem perplexes you?"

She nipped at her lip a bit, then looked up into his eyes. "I realized this morning after our meeting in the library that something must be done about Neville *before* he falls into some kind of trouble, no matter how innocent. I fear he has far too much time on his hands."

"And what have you decided? Should we send him to Oxford or the Naval College, as he suggested?"

She lowered her gaze to her hands, fidgeting with the ties to her cloak. "Either would be expensive, and we have no right to impose on you, sir. Besides, Uncle Philippe is Neville's guardian. He would have to be consulted about any decision that would entail my brother leaving the Chase."

Alexander hadn't realized Lady Landry had no true power over the Rochelles save the ability to take away the roof over their heads. With his arrival, he'd removed even that bit of power. He straightened and looked out over the tops of the trees at the windmill standing silhouetted against the darkening sky.

"I think we can safely assume your uncle would prefer his heir to be ensconced in the ivy towers of Oxford instead of dashing about the marshes at night."

Valara gasped indignantly. "I didn't mean to imply Neville was involved with that business last night."

Alexander's eyes narrowed as they remained fixed on

the windmill. Something about the structure seemed different, but he couldn't put his finger on it. He suddenly felt the young lady's hand on his arm, and he drew his gaze away to stare into her amazing blue eyes.

"Do *you* think my brother is involved with smugglers?" There was more fear than anger in her voice.

"I don't know for certain, Miss Rochelle. Someone at the manor is involved with something clandestine, and I fully intend to find out who it is and what he is doing. Then I shall take appropriate measures."

In the fading light, it looked almost as if Valara's face grew ashen. "You must do what you think is proper. I-it grows late, and I must go see if my aunt or cousin has need of me." The young lady turned and hurried away from him.

Alexander stood watching the place were she had disappeared around the turn in the roof. Clearly she was afraid her brother would be found to be involved. He could do little to reassure her until after tonight. Then all uncertainty would be at an end—he hoped.

Setting about the business at hand, he surveyed the grounds at the rear of the manor. With Roger's help, they would be able to cover the east and west side of the building. The denseness of the trees and the darkness almost certainly would force the man to stick with the paths that had been worn through the woods. Alex felt certain they would discover the identity of the culprit tonight.

Five

Darkness lay like a black shroud over Landry Chase as the denizens of the forest scurried from their nests and burrows to begin their nightly routine of foraging. Yet the two gentlemen who slipped into the inky night paid little heed to the resident wildlife. Alexander led the way to a cluster of birches that lay off the west rear corner of the manor.

The men quickly reached the consuming shadows of the trees unseen. Sir Roger took up a position, then stared at the rear of the manor, which loomed like a black mountain in the darkness. "I swear it's darker than the inside of a cow's stomach, Alex. We shall never be able to see a thing."

The baron chuckled softly as he glanced over his shoulder, where not a single beam of light glowed. "You've spent too many nights in well-lit, comfortable drawing rooms, my friend. I assure you once your eyes accustom themselves to the darkness you can see well enough." He didn't add, *especially when your life depends upon it,* as his had in the Peninsula.

"Do you think the Gentlemen will be out and about two nights in a row?" Sir Roger leaned against the trunk of the tree, ever watchful of the house.

"My guess is they are active most moonless nights.

Besides, if the dragoons discovered the Gentlemen last night, likely they had to hide the casks and run. Whoever is involved will need to move the goods inland. If someone at the Chase is helping move the brandy, they will have to pass by you or me. I locked the front door and the library doors." Alexander patted his pocket, where he'd put the keys. "The only way out is through the rear doors. If you spot him, wait till he passes, then give the signal and I'll come. I will do the same should I spot him."

Alexander stepped out of the shadows, intending to move to a position at the opposite side of the building.

At that moment, the distant screech of old hinges echoed softly on the night air. He ducked back into the blackness and waited. Within minutes, a figure separated from the darkness of the building, heading west at a rapid gait.

Surprised that their quarry was so early, Alexander lingered just long enough for the shadowy figure to pass. Then he quietly signaled Sir Roger to follow. A sinking feeling burned in Alex's chest as he peered closely at the person silhouetted against the night sky. There could be little doubt the willowy figure was Neville Rochelle.

Alex knew an immediate impulse to grab the boy by his collar and drag him back to the manor, ringing a peal over him the entire way. The boy's sister would be devastated if anything happened to him. But earlier Alex had decided to trail anyone who departed the manor. He didn't want any false excuses for why a man was out and about in the night. That required catching the culprit with the goods.

Mr. Rochelle crossed the gardens and disappeared into the woods that surrounded Landry Chase. The men picked up their pace, fearful they would lose him among the dense trees. To their amazement, Neville appeared not the least concerned he might be followed, for he marched along at a steady pace, making a surprising bit of noise stepping on dead leaves and fallen limbs.

After nearly fifteen minutes of brisk walking, the young man was again in open pasture land. His dark figure stood out against the grassy meadow as he continued on his chosen path. Alex halted at the tree line to allow Neville to put some distance between them, for if they could see him, then should he look over his shoulder, he would be able to see them.

"Where the devil do you think the lad is going?" Sir Roger whispered, as they waited for the boy to climb a stone fence and disappear on the other side. "We must have walked inland over a mile from the coast."

"He's just left Landry lands, so I haven't a clue to his destination." Alexander and Sir Roger set off to follow once again.

As they scaled the stone fence, they could just make out Neville as he entered the woods some distance away on the far side of the road. They hurried across the rutted lane and plunged into the forest, just barely able to discern a path in the burgeoning new growth of spring. Once again the cluster of trees ended, but this time the men halted to survey a dark towering structure that loomed in the clearing before them.

Alexander pulled his friend to a squat on the ground behind a small fir tree when he heard the drumming of a rapidly moving horse in the distance. "I think we are at the rendezvous point. These crumbled ruins might hold the secret."

Sir Roger peered round the needles of the small tree at the roofless building that time had ravaged. The window panes were long gone, but the lovely arched frames still stood, regally announcing its sacred origins. "It's an old Saxon church. One would have thought the Riding Officer would have looked here first."

At that precise moment, a gray horse came into view, a cloaked rider on its is back. The visitor rode straight to the ruins, then slid effortlessly to the ground. After throwing the reins over the limb of a small tree, the new arrival disappeared into the front arch of the round tower.

Moments later a light appeared, illuminating the arches with a ghostly yellow glow, as if an angel had returned to visit the holy building.

Sir Roger leaned forward and whispered, "These are not the brightest of smugglers to be calling attention to themselves in such a manner."

Alexander stared thoughtfully at the soft yellow glow pouring from the front arch. "These woods will cloak the light, as they do the ruins. 'Tis possible Waite doesn't even know this hull of a church is here, since we are on private land and several miles from the sea. But I think what we have stumbled upon is a tryst and nothing more sinister. Unless I miss my guess, that was a female."

The baronet rocked back on his heels, nearly toppling over before he grabbed the nearest limb to steady himself. "Are you telling me that slip of a lad is involved in some kind of love affair?"

"There is only one way to find out. We shall give them a few minutes to make their greetings, then confront Neville and his paramour. Shall we take a peek from that side door?"

Inside the moss coated walls of the old Saxon ruin, Neville remained totally unaware he had been under observation since he'd left the manor. His thoughts had been too consumed with seeing his beautiful Bly once again. She'd failed him last night, but perhaps her brother had intercepted the note he'd sent over by old Jonas or she'd been unable to slip away.

What had been far worse was he'd almost gotten caught by that fool Waite, who'd been roving about searching for smugglers. Neville shook his head to think that anyone could mistake him for such a fool as to involve himself in something so dangerous.

The sound of hoofbeats echoed, and Neville jumped down from the stone boulder he'd been waiting on. He fumbled in the dark alcove for the tinderbox and candles he'd brought the day before, wondering how much Bly might have changed since he'd seen her two years ago. He'd had only moments to declare his devotion at their final parting here so long ago.

The candle flamed to life, and he used it to light several more. Neville turned to find her standing just inside the doorway of the sanctuary. His heart seemed to jump in his chest, for she was more beautiful than he remembered. A soft breeze whispered through the open ruins, causing the candles to flicker as if her image were a mere illusion. She stepped toward him.

"You haven't changed a bit, Neville." Her tone was one of disappointment, as if she'd expected him to have grown to full manhood in the years since her departure.

Something strange seemed to prick at his confidence as he drank in her beauty. Despite the same raven locks and clear blue eyes, this was not the girl of two years ago with tumbled curls and men's breeches. This was not his Bly, but instead Lady Blythe, sister of the Earl of Westoke. Her fashionable maroon riding habit, half covered by a black cape, exhibited a figure grown shapely. The set of her full lips seemed almost bored and her manner not quite cold, but condescending.

"Neville, have you not yet outgrown these foolish games of our youth?" She drew off her riding gloves. "I couldn't believe my eyes when I read your note. We are surely long past such pranks as galloping about the marshes at night."

He suddenly felt like a child. Glad of the dim candlelight that concealed his warm cheeks, Neville shrugged.

"You know your brother would not have allowed me to visit you openly at Westwood. He made it clear he thought we at the Chase might lead you astray." He paused for a moment before he asked, "Have you been well since going away to school?"

Appearing far more interested in surveying the interior of the ruin than in her companion, she picked up an engraved stone as she replied, "I was bored, dreadfully bored, but I did have the last three months in Bath with my aunt, Lady Ashley. I do so adore the theater and parties. Westoke promised me a Season, but I think he was hoping I would make a match in Bath so he didn't have to foot the bill for London." She gave a wicked laugh. "I intend to be the reigning beauty this Season once we go to Town." She turned her face to him and looked up through her lashes. "Do you think I can?"

"You have a mirror, my lady," Neville replied stiffly. She was ravishing, but at the moment she appeared a stranger. A sophisticated, flirtatious creature had taken his Bly's place. He'd been a fool to think things wouldn't change after so long.

The young man was so lost in his shattered dreams that he failed to give the proper response to a young lady, who of late was used to being fawned over by the young men of Bath. Instead of seeing admiration, all that was evident was total bewilderment on Neville's face. Lady Blythe, spoiled though she'd become, was woman enough to realize he still harbored their old dreams of romance. Then it dawned upon the young woman that Neville Rochelle might be the only gentleman left in the neighborhood to admire her, at least until she went to London.

With an artful glance, she determined to test her new-found abilities to flirt and make him fall under her spell. She stepped forward and planted a kiss on his cheek. "Oh, Nev, you are such a delightful innocent to think things would be the same after being parted for so long. I am quite grown up and cannot engage in foolish adventures on the marshes or even a little romance. I must think of my reputation. You will see what I mean once you are not marooned here in Norfolk. Why, you must demand to be allowed to go to London and acquire some Town bronze. I shall insist Westoke invite you to my coming out ball. I feel—" She halted mid-sentence. Her beautiful eyes widened as she looked over her shoulder. "What was that noise?"

"I heard nothing." Neville, savoring the feel of her hands on his arm and the smell of her French perfume, was oblivious to all but his companion, as he again began to fall under the spell of this beautiful creature before him.

Lady Blythe rapidly donned her gloves. "I must go. If Westoke found I had come, he might delay my Season." She hurried to the door, then paused and looked back over her shoulder. "I quite forgot to ask how things are at the Chase with the new baron. I believe Lady Landry said his mother was an Italian actress or some such. Is he rather vulgar?"

Stung by the implied insult to a man he was coming to admire, Neville snapped, "Lord Landry is a proper gentleman. How dare you repeat such gossip—"

From a side door in the old ruin, his lordship's voice sliced into what could become a lover's spat. "Perhaps your friend would like to meet me herself."

The young lady gasped at being caught in such an improper situation. Without a word, she turned and dashed into the darkness. Moments later, the clatter of her mount's hooves announced her departure.

Neville stood frozen with shock. "Lord Landry, w-what are you doing here?"

"Following you." Alexander stepped into the full glow of the candles as he peered round the interior of the church. Sir Roger remained at the door, crossing his arms and watching Neville bemusedly.

The baron picked his way among the fallen masonry to the door where the young lady had just departed, then looked back at the frightened young man. "I acquit you of being a smuggler, my boy, which I own is a great relief. But what can you be thinking to involve a young lady in such an improper dalliance? Can I assume that was Lady Blythe, of whom you spoke earlier?"

The boy looked positively hunted. "You won't tell anyone about this, will you? I already have enough black marks in my book in her brother's mind. He would never allow me to see her again if he learns about this meeting."

Alexander eyed the boy thoughtfully. He'd known young love himself. He remembered a dark Spanish beauty who'd held him entranced for a year until she'd run off and married the heir of a viscount. He'd suffered nearly a month until the next beautiful female crossed his path. It was the way with young men. "Sir Roger and I shan't betray you. But in return you must promise me that you will see the young lady only at properly chaperoned affairs."

"But—"

Alex held up his hand. "I shall do my best to smooth the waters with the earl, to convince him you and the others have outgrown your foolish pranks. After that, it will be in your hands to court the lady. Agreed?"

A rather dubious look settled on the boy's face. Still, he had little choice. "I agree."

"Then shall we return to the Chase before Captain Waite stumbles across us and tumbles us all into the gaol with charges of smuggling? Am I right in assuming it was you he ran across last night?"

"Yes, Alexander."

The baron sighed with relief. The mystery was solved. "Shall we return to the Chase?"

As the men made their way back to the manor, Alexander felt certain he could now put all his efforts into repairing the estate, since this problem had been safely put to rest.

Valara tugged her cloak tighter as she stepped from the safety of the woods and hurried across the meadow toward the mill tower. The building was a black monolith against the star-flecked sky. It was fortunate she had no fear of the darkness, for too often she had been forced to come to the mill during the night to retrieve Uncle Philippe's messages.

Her aunt's incessant demands from her sickbed had kept Valara from slipping away during the afternoon to leave her letter in the empty space behind the mill's sign. She'd hated deceiving Lady Landry from the beginning, but secrecy was of the utmost importance. The dust had barely settled at Waterloo when her uncle Philippe had paid his final visit and asked for her help. He'd been approached by a member of the Bourbon court who was working with an agent of the English prime minister. The men offered an opportunity for Philippe to do his country and England, where he'd resided for years, a service. His efforts would protect the monarchy of France from Bonaparte's loyal followers. For his mission to succeed, he'd need Valara's help.

The *comte* had assured his niece there would be nothing dangerous in what she would do. She knew his life depended on her ability to hold her tongue and to pass the messages. While at the Chase on an earlier visit, her uncle had befriended Mr. Akers and knew of his pigeons. Philippe had brought birds with him to use and the young man had gladly offered to house them at his dovecote. Akers didn't know what the birds carried, but he willingly helped Valara send her messages to London, thinking the young lady and her uncle bird fanciers as well.

The information being sent regarded the various plots Uncle Philippe uncovered to return Napoleon to the throne of France. The English, who very much wanted to keep the man in exile, in turn dispatched the information to Louis XVIII's government so the would-be conspirators could be arrested. The country of her ancestors remained deeply divided between the Royalists and the old Republicans.

She'd never confided in Neville about her monthly visits to the mill after dark. There could be little doubt he would want to take over the business, stranded as he was in this remote estate and longing to do something—anything—of interest. But there had been no problems over the months that she'd passed the notes.

On the roof this evening, she hadn't been surprised when she'd seen the signal from the tower that the Frenchmen could land safely tonight. She never questioned who unfurled the mill's sail, not wanting to involve herself with the smugglers, but she was always alert to the Gentlemen's activities, knowing she must look for a new message during the dark of the moon. She'd been afraid for a moment that Lord Landry had seen the signal, but she'd managed to distract him.

She clutched her own letter tightly in her hand. It was rare that she sent her uncle a missive, and she hoped she could be in time before the courier put Philippe's report in the hollow space. She wanted to inform her uncle of Lord Landry's offer to send Neville to school. She supported the idea and wanted to send her brother away to keep him out of trouble. She'd also demanded to know when Uncle Philippe's masquerade would be at an end. She held hopes he might eventually be able to summon Neville to France and a future, which he wouldn't have here in Norfolk as the impoverished nephew of Lady Landry.

As she moved stealthily across the open field, she realized Waite was making it far too dangerous for her to be out and about in the marshes at night. While she didn't involve herself in the free-trade, she did depend on the Gentlemen to keep up her line of communication with her uncle. Unfortunately, the Riding Officer was determined to catch someone, and after last night he suspected someone from the Chase. But whoever had been out last night, it certainly hadn't been her.

Now Lord Landry was involved. The meeting with his lordship on the roof had left her a bit unnerved. He was equally determined to know the identity of the mysterious person, and his investigation might inadvertently stumble across her activities. She could only pray it hadn't been Neville. Whatever would she do if her brother got them tossed from the their home just because he'd let boredom entice him into trouble?

Gravel crunched under her feet as she came to the mill's front door. It seemed unduly noisy in the stillness of the meadow, and she paused to listen for the hue and cry from the dragoons. The wind was low, and there was only the soft sound of waves lapping against the rocks that dotted the beach. To her relief, all remained silent. Then a strange feeling come over her, like she was being watched. She looked over her shoulder, but could see nothing save the empty, grass-covered dunes.

Deciding she was merely on edge from her worries about Neville, she turned and lifted the weathered sign carved with the words Landry Chase Mill. It made a mild screech as the hinges protested. She reached in and found the alcove empty. The courier hadn't been there yet. Relieved, she shoved her own message into the box.

A hand shot out from the dark recess of the doorway, trapping Valara's wrist. She gasped as she was dragged inside the mill and the door slammed shut behind her. The odor of brandy and dead fish choked her as she struggled to free herself. The grip loosened on her hand, and the glare of a lantern being unshuttered made her blink. Her captor moved back into the golden glow of the light and she got a good look at the man. Coarse featured and weather-beaten, the bearded man grinned at her, exposing his few remaining teeth.

"Ah, *mademoiselle*, at last I meet Jacques's *Anglais* friend. A pretty one at that."

Valara's heart froze. She knew her uncle was using the name Jacques Montaine in France. If this man didn't know Philippe's real name, it likely meant he couldn't be trusted. The leer in his eyes sent a shiver down her spine. She must give him no clue as to her relationship to the man he knew.

"How dare you accost me? *Monsieur* Montaine will cut out your heart if I tell him how I was treated." She wondered if the man could hear her heart pounding as she did her best to play a spoiled, arrogant Englishwoman.

"But he es not here." The man's eyes glittered menacingly. At last he chuckled and shook his head. "Do not look so frightened, *mon petite*, I, Jean Dubois, want money, not your . . . how do you *Anglais* say, your virtue."

Valara gave a shuddering sigh of relief, but she knew she was far from safe. "Money? Did not *monsieur* pay you to bring me a message?"

The sailor picked up the lantern. "He es without zee funds at zee moment and wants you to pay me, *hein*? He has zee important message I must bring on my next trip in four days."

"But I haven't any money either." Where would she find money to pay this man?

A screech echoed in the distance that might have been a human or a gull. One couldn't tell through the thick wall of the mill. Without a word, Jean jerked the shutter back over the lantern and the interior of the mill fell into darkness. Moments later the door opened and his large bulk stood silhouetted against the starlit sky. "If zere es no money in zee box when next I come"—he tapped the sign where she'd put her letter—"zen I don't deliver his message." With those ominous words, the man strode into the darkness.

Valara rushed to the door. "I shall find the money somehow."

She watched him until his dark shape disappeared over the dunes, her mind in turmoil with where she would find the money. Then she realized he hadn't taken her message to her uncle. But it really didn't matter that Philippe didn't receive her letter if she couldn't find the funds to pay the man.

Should she send a message to London? She doubted the gentleman who received the messages would send any funds since he didn't know her, nor she him. No, she must find some other way to come by the money.

Her next thought was to turn to Lord Landry for help, but she pushed that from her mind, wondering what could have made her think of him. She and her brother had too much to lose, and there could be little doubt that Lord Landry strongly disapproved of smuggling, not to mention the dangerous business she had become entangled with. He might think that to be using the smugglers to transport messages was just as reprehensible as importing brandy.

The only person she would trust to help her besides Neville, who hadn't a feather to fly with either, was Ellie. Perhaps if she knew what was involved, she might have some idea where Valara could find the funds to pay off Dubois.

Valara would have to reveal what she had been about to her cousin, but she didn't fear the girl would betray her. More likely Ellie would throw herself into the clandestine operation wholeheartedly, as she did with most things she thought an adventure.

Suddenly a shout of discovery echoed on the breeze, bringing Valara out of her musings with frightening speed. Waite and his men were running up the beach. She dashed across the open meadow, heedless of any unseen obstacles that might lie in her dark path. Reaching the woods safely, she sped as rapidly as she could down the familiar path back to the manor. Her heart raced as she heard running footsteps behind her.

The towering silhouette of the manor was a welcome sight as she exited the trees. She ran full tilt across the lawn, her skirts lifted, and slipped into the kitchen. She shut the portal and turned the lock. Leaning against the oaken door, she gasped for breath.

That had been too close. Not only would she have ruined their situation at the Chase had she been caught, but she would likely have cost her uncle his life as well. That didn't bear thinking about.

After several minutes, when she once again breathed at a normal pace, she made her way up to her room. She prayed her uncle's work was nearly at an end. If he had no money, likely he would be forced to return. All she knew for certain was that she must find the funds Dubois wanted and put them in the alcove.

At the top of the stairs, she stopped to listen when she thought she heard masculine voices below stairs. Was it the servants, or were his lordship and his friend still in the library? Whatever happened, she didn't want Lord Landry to learn about her excursion tonight. She couldn't risk having him take back his offer to send Neville safely away to school and demand they leave the

Chase. Not wanting to be discovered by anyone, she hurried down the hall to her room.

The following morning, Elaina's fork clattered to her plate as she stared across the breakfast table at her cousin. "You mean you have been running about on the marshes at night for months and didn't let me go with you?"

Before Valara could respond, the door to the breakfast parlor opened and the new kitchen maid, Beth, stepped into the room, bringing a new pot of coffee. Valara thanked her, then waited until she and her cousin were alone again before she said, "This isn't some silly game, Ellie. If something goes wrong, my uncle might lose his life. The men he must associate with think I am his English paramour whose parents have forbidden a match. If they found out he's my uncle and is sending information about their plots, they wouldn't hesitate to kill him. Their allegiance to Napoleon is that strong."

Elaina picked up her fork, but did not resume eating. After a moment, she looked up at her cousin. "Forgive me. I didn't mean to make light of the situation. I merely long for a little adventure, instead of sitting here under Mama's thumb waiting for Westoke to come up to scratch." Her voice held no joy at that prospect. She put down her fork without taking a bite. "You will need money to pay this man, and with that I can help."

Valara's brows rose. "You have funds Uncle Bart didn't know about?"

"Hardly. No, I have a lovely pearl necklace my godmother gave me years ago. I think Papa had quite forgotten about it, or it would have been sold to the jeweler like all of Mama's lovely gems. I don't know its value, but it should do the trick. There is a small shop on a side street in Cley where we might sell the necklace. If we hurry, we can go to town and back before Mama wakes. She need never know what we have done."

Valara reached across the table and squeezed her cousin's hand. "I don't know how, but I promise my uncle will repay you for your help."

Elaina tilted her head. "Promise you will let me help you, should you have a need at some future time. You know you don't have to face this alone."

After only a moment's hesitation, Valara nodded her head. "I promise, and thank you."

The young ladies finished their breakfast then went upstairs to retrieve their coats, bonnets, and Elaina's necklace, which had been safely hidden in a small drawer in a Queen Anne secretaire. They stood in the front hall drawing on their gloves when the front door opened to reveal Lord Landry and Sir Roger returning from their morning ride. Valara thought both gentlemen extremely handsome in their riding gear, but her gaze was drawn to Alexander, as her brother had taken to calling the gentleman. The baron seemed in a surprisingly good mood as he smiled at them both and doffed his beaver hat.

"Good morning, ladies." His lordship eyed their attire. "Are you going out for a walk so early?"

"We are, sir," Elaina calmly acknowledged when Valara stood mute, appearing unable to draw her gaze from the baron's smiling face.

After a moment of silence, Sir Roger asked, "May we . . . join you?" His tone held a fear of rejection.

The young ladies exchanged a worried look before Valara, regaining her composure, admitted, "We are walking all the way to Cley to do some shopping. I don't think—"

"Cley. I have yet to visit the village." Lord Landry's smile widened. "Would you ladies object if we accompanied you? I shall order the carriage and save you the long walk."

Wanting desperately to say no, Valara's fear of discovery melted away as the man's gaze seemed to warm her. She savored the feeling for a moment before she remembered why they were going to the village. "T-truly there is little to see, my lord." When the smiling light dimmed in his amber eyes, she weakened and in a rush added, "But we would welcome your company."

Elaina stepped on Valara's toe in warning, but she didn't care. She couldn't bring herself to be deliberately rude to someone who'd only been kind to her and her brother. It was soon settled that the four would go to Cley-next-the-Sea, and the gentlemen escorted the ladies to the stables.

While they waited for the grooms to harness the team, Lord Landry edged Valara a bit away from his friend and cousin. "Miss Rochelle, I wanted to ease your worries about Neville by reassuring you your brother is not involved with smugglers."

"You are certain, my lord?" Hopeful, she took a step forward.

"I have put my doubts to rest, as should you."

Despite the good news, Valara couldn't relax. Her mind returned to the problem of the man at the mill. She fidgeted with the strings of her reticule, knowing she'd been a fool to invite Lord Landry to go with them. His presence might well prevent them from being able to sell Ellie's necklace. Seeing his lordship watching her, she forced a nervous smile and returned to the subject at hand. "What eased your doubts, my lord?"

"I discovered his nocturnal wanderings are because he is in love."

His words penetrated her distraction, and Valara's brow wrinkled a moment. Then her eyes widened. "Good grief, don't tell me he is still mooning after Lady

Blythe Crane! That was mere puppy love when they were little more than children. He must know Lord Westoke would never consent to a match between them."

"His mind may know, but his heart hasn't listened. I suspect his feelings would have faded in the course of time had he other females to distract him, but due to his isolation he's been stranded here with no one to capture his interest. I fear he's allowed a childhood romance to blossom into something it is not—at least not on the lady's part."

With all the possibilities of what Lord Westoke could do to her brother if he should cross the earl, Valara made a decision. "My lord, I should like to take you up on your offer to send Neville to school, i-if it won't be too much of an expense. I am certain my uncle would approve."

Lord Landry nodded. "I shall write to my solicitor once Neville tells me whether he prefers Oxford or Naval College. But you do understand it will be some time before all the arrangements can be made. You shall have plenty of time to consult with your uncle on the matter."

"I understand, and thank you for being so kind." She sighed with relief. "Surely knowing he is to go will do much to keep his romantic urges in check." This she said as much to herself as to his lordship.

His lordship merely chuckled. "We can only hope so."

At last the carriage was ready and the four travelers climbed in. To Valara's surprise, Elaina openly flirted with Sir Roger all the way to Cley. Valara suspected it was done out of boredom, for there could be little doubt her cousin was well aware of Lady Landry's opinion of Sir Roger.

Valara remained silent through much of the journey,

her mind at a loss as to how they would accomplish their task and not alert Lord Landry to her involvement with the gentlemen. But would he disapprove of something that was for the good of England? More likely he would disapprove because she, a mere female, was involved.

She peered up at him through her lashes and noted that he watched his cousin's coquetting with a slight frown. He seemed to dislike Ellie's conduct, or perhaps he thought she was only toying with his friend. She knew so little of him, it was difficult to determine what his expression meant. She had far more important things to worry about at the moment, and she turned her attention out the window.

The small harbor town of Cley teemed with people on most mornings, and today was no different. Several ships had anchored during the night, and the Customs House was busy as the goods were unloaded. Stacked crates of English wool sat on the quay, ready to be put on board as soon as the ships took on new cargo.

His lordship's carriage drew up in front of the King's Arms, a small inn near the village mill. The young ladies had barely stepped from the carriage when Elaina whispered, "Lead them down to the quay. With all that is going on, I should be able to slip away and sell the necklace."

As Valara turned, Lord Landry extended his arm to her. She blushed, as much from guilt as shyness, but lightly touched her hand to his sleeve and allowed him to escort her down the street. Their progress was slow, for there was much curiosity about the new baron, and many of the locals stopped to speak with the young ladies, hoping for introductions.

At last they arrived at the hustle and bustle of the stone landing and stood taking in the teeming scene.

Valara began to chatter nervously, not knowing what else to do to distract the gentlemen. "During much of the last ten years, Cley has had difficult times, what with Napoleon controlling nearly all of the continental ports on the North Sea, but they managed to keep trade going with Russia. Since '13, when Prince William regained control of Holland, most of what is brought in comes from the Low Countries." She gestured to a ship that flew the flag of the House of Orange. "Dutch cheese, fruit, and flowers, but more recently, with France's defeat, there are again ships from France bringing fabrics and wine."

Before his lordship or Sir Roger could comment, a loud crash sounded some distance down the landing, drawing their attention. A crate being unloaded had tumbled to the quay, and apples began to spill out of one side. In an instant, several small boys rushed forward and snatched up the red fruit, then as quickly disappeared into the crowd of sailors and fishermen. A burly seaman roared and gave chase to one small lad with an apple in each hand. The boy's short legs weren't sufficient to outrun the larger man.

Scarcely five feet in front of where Valara and the others watched, the sailor overtook the boy, grabbing his collar and lifting him entirely off the dock. "I've got ye, ye wharf rat! Give me them apples." He shook the lad roughly, then looked about. "Where's the beadle? I'll see ye locked up, ye little thief."

The towheaded urchin's terrified gaze locked on the pretty lady in black, and recognition dawned. With a childish wail, he cried, "Miss Rochelle, don't be lettin' 'im send me to the gaol!"

Valara's stomach plummeted as she realized the man held little Henry Dodd from Seaforth Orphanage. He was one of the boys she'd been teaching to write his letters for the past six weeks. Unlike some of the others, he'd shown a sharp mind. Without a thought for anything else, she advanced on the seaman, who continued to shake the lad, as if hoping to rattle the apples from the boy's grasp.

"Put that child down at once!" Valara moved to stand in front of the burly man, her arms akimbo.

" 'E's none but a thief, miss, and ye needn't worry yer 'ead about 'im."

"Henry's only a child. Put him down." She reached out to grasp one of the boy's arms.

The sailor's jaw set in a stubborn line. "The lad's got to learn what 'appen's to thievin' culls."

Lord Landry's deep voice washed over Valara as he stepped to her side. "You *will* put the boy down. At once, my good fellow."

"And 'ose goin' to pay for these 'ere apples?" The seaman lowered Henry's feet back to the dock, but he never released his hold on the boy's collar while he eyed the tall gentleman, who had a steely glint in his amber eyes.

Sir Roger stepped up to the other side of Valara. "This fruit should be listed as damaged in shipping." The baronet reached out his hand to Henry, and the boy reluctantly surrendered one of the apples. Holding up the fruit and pointing to a wide gash that glowed whitely against the red skin, Sir Roger said, "This gash will render the fruit inedible by afternoon. Any market peddler would have to throw it away. It was ruined when it fell from the crate and is therefore useless."

The seaman's eyes narrowed as he looked from one gentry cove to the other. The man knew a lost cause when he saw one. He released his hold on the boy. "It ain't right, but who am I to argue with the likes of ye?"

"That's a good fellow." Lord Landry flipped a coin to the seaman, who grabbed it from the air, then turned and walked away, still grumbling about thievin' lads.

Valara knelt down, taking Henry by the arms. "Whatever are you doing here at the quay? You might have been hurt—or worse."

The blond lad shuffled his feet a moment as he stared at the ground. "I just came to see the new ships what come in last night, miss. I didn't mean no 'arm. When I seen them other lads grab those apples, I 'ad a 'ankerin' for one meself."

The baron knelt beside Valara. "Henry, Miss Rochelle isn't likely to be around to pull you out of trouble the next time. You wouldn't want to end up in the gaol for something so simple as an apple, would you?"

The young lad's eyes grew wide as he stared into his lordship's face. "Do ye want me to give 'em back, sir? I don't want to be makin' trouble for Miss Rochelle. She's an angel come to earth." The child's gaze roved to Valara's face and held such a moonstruck look she had to stifle a laugh even as her cheeks warmed.

Lord Landry's mouth twitched, but he managed to maintain his composure. "As Sir Roger said, this apple is damaged and must be eaten at once or it will go bad, so you may have it."

A smile lit Henry's face and he took a large bite from the apple he still held.

Valara and the baron rose, but she put out her hand and ruffled the boy's blond hair. "Promise me there will be no more taking things you find on the quay."

The lad nodded his head as he munched his treat.

"Very good, Henry. Now I think you should return to Seaforth before Mr. Binion discovers you have gone." Seeing the frown settle on the lad's face, she added, "Or before that seaman changes his mind about finding the beadle to take you into custody."

Henry glanced over his shoulder. Then he nodded and muttered, "Right ye are, Miss Rochelle."

As he was about to depart, Sir Roger called to him. "Wait, take the rest of your booty as well, my little pirate." He tossed the apple back to young Henry, who snatched it from the air and beamed at the prospect of two such treats in one day.

Henry looked at Miss Rochelle, then held up the second apple. "A is for apple." With a cheeky laugh, he ran off up the main street of Cley.

Valara and the others, watching him disappear into the crowd, laughed. When Lord Landry turned to his friend to remark on the lad's pluck, Valara suddenly realized Elaina had managed to slip away unnoticed by the gentlemen. She breathed a sigh of relief. By this evening she would have the money she needed for the Frenchman at the mill.

"Miss Rochelle!" a surly voice called from down the docks. "I must speak with you at once."

Valara turned to see Captain Waite striding purposefully toward her through the seamen busy at work. Her heart froze. Despite the distance, the Riding Officer's gaze never left her face. It held such animosity that a shiver ran down her spine. There could be little doubt he must have seen her last night and was about to unmask her here in front of Lord Landry and everyone. She closed her eyes a moment as the world began to spin.

Six

By chance, Alexander turned to ask Miss Rochelle about the little urchin at the same time Waite shouted her name. A look of sheer terror flashed across the lady's face, and her cheeks blanched. Then her eyes fluttered and she began to sway. He reached out and grabbed her, thinking her about to crumple to the stone quay.

"Are you unwell, Miss Rochelle?"

The young lady's trembling hand came to her brow. "I—I think the heat is a bit much for me, my lord. Could we go to the inn and have something cool to drink?"

The weather was very mild that morning, to Alex's way of thinking, but he knew females were far more delicate. Or was she trying to avoid the obnoxious Captain Waite? Whatever the reason, Alex knew she needed to leave. "Come, we shall go at once."

He looked up to summon the others. Of Elaina there was no sign, but he signaled his friend, who'd fallen into conversation with a ship's officer. "Roger, where is my cousin?"

The gentleman's brows rose as he realized the young lady was nowhere to be seen. "She was here just a moment ago." His gaze searched up and down the quay for the young lady before Miss Rochelle stopped him.

"She has gone to run an errand, sir. She shall come to no harm and will be back presently."

"She went unaccompanied?" There was a hint of censure in Sir Roger's tone, but his face was more telling. He had the look of a wounded puppy because the lady hadn't requested his company.

Miss Rochelle nodded. "We have not had the luxury of an excess of footmen or grooms, sir. I do assure you, we are quite used to going about on our own. Besides, everyone in and about Cley knows who my cousin is and would never accost her. It is a simple errand, and she will return soon quite safe."

Angry at Elaina's lack of consideration, Alexander put his hand under Miss Rochelle's arm and began to guide her back up the stone landing toward the inn. "No doubt my headstrong cousin shall be able to find her way back to the inn as well, since that is where the carriage waits." Looking back over his shoulder, he noted that the Riding Officer had been stopped by one of the Customs House men, but the soldier continued to watch the departing party from the Chase. Alexander wondered what Waite could have to say to them, since there was now no doubt that Neville was innocent—but then the soldier didn't know that.

In a matter of minutes after arriving at the King's Arms, the baron had Miss Rochelle safely ensconced in a private parlor, sipping apple cider. Sir Roger had volunteered to remain outside on the watch for Miss Addington. But within minutes a knock sounded on the door and Captain Waite stepped into the room.

"I must speak with Miss Rochelle at once."

Alexander was prepared for him. He stepped into the man's path, halting his entry into the room. "The young lady is unwell. You may discuss whatever you wish with me."

Miss Rochelle gamely rose. "I am feeling better and shall hear what Captain Waite has to say, sir."

Alexander eyed her a moment and noted there was more color in her cheeks. "Very well." He stepped aside, and the soldier moved across the small, low-beamed parlor.

The Riding Officer directed his comments to the young lady. "I've come to tell you I nearly caught young Mr. Neville last night as he fled his meeting at the mill. I warned both you and Lord Landry what the boy was about and you both—"

"Captain Waite!" the baron interrupted as he leaned back against the doorjamb, crossing his arms over his chest. "I happen to know young Mr. Rochelle was nowhere near the mill last night."

The officer jutted out his chin as he turned to his lordship. "And just how can you know that, my lord? I happened to be at the mill and saw him flee into the woods."

"I don't know who you saw, sir, but it was not Neville. I was with the boy until nearly one in the morning, and neither of us were at the mill." Seeing doubt fill Waite's eyes, Alexander added, "I wanted to know for certain the boy wasn't in league with the Gentlemen, and I attained my proof last night."

The captain's mouth pursed thoughtfully. "Well then, my lord, all that means is that I had the wrong bird in my sights. I was hot on the trail of someone who left the mill in a hurry, and I'd swear he entered Landry Chase or vanished into thin air." Waite crossed his own arms. "And I'm not a believer in sorcery or black magic."

"Nor am I, Captain." Alexander grew thoughtful and glanced at Miss Rochelle, but her face was a blank mask. "You cannot think my butler or that old footman, Jonas, is larking about on the marshes, can you?"

Waite shook his head. "Hardly, my lord. It's been my

experience that free-trading is generally an occupation of the young." The soldier seemed to go into a brown study. Then his face took on a look of discovery. "Well, if it ain't Rochelle, the next most likely candidate would be your cousin. She has a reputation for being a very unconventional and adventuresome miss. Or haven't you heard about her taking a crate of Mr. Akers's birds to the ruins at Cromer and letting them go?"

"Heavens, Captain Waite," Miss Rochelle snapped, coming out of her stupor to valiantly defend her cousin. "Elaina was scarcely more than a child when she did that, and all Mr. Akers's birds returned to the dovecote, just as he'd always said they would. You cannot think she would still be doing such things now that she is grown. My cousin may be a bit headstrong, but she would never break the law."

"What I see is a high-spirited female with little to occupy her."

Valara Rochelle's mouth pursed in frustration as she turned to his lordship. "Don't believe him, sir. Perhaps you should know the captain is known for his rash speculations about free-traders. All he has accused have proven to be innocent."

Alexander knew he must do something to put an end to the man's speculation about his cousin.

"Captain Waite." His lordship stepped toward the Riding Officer, an angry glint in his amber eyes. "I hope I don't need to remind you I would take it badly if I were to hear my cousin's name bandied about in such a manner in Cley without the least proof."

The officer stepped back as he saw something in the new baron's face that caused him to straighten and look decidedly less assured. After several moments of indecision, Waite marched to the door, then halted. "I am only doing my job, and I must go where the clues lead me." With that, he exited the room.

Alexander turned back to see Miss Rochelle sag into her chair. Suspicion ran rife in his chest. "Now that we are alone, pray tell me my cousin has not been so utterly foolish as to involve herself with a band of cutthroat smugglers."

The young lady's cheeks flamed pink. "Have you seen evidence anyone at the Chase has been enjoying the fruits of money earned from smuggling, Lord Landry?"

There could be little doubt no such evidence existed. From the kitchens to the drawing rooms, there were only signs of privation. "Perhaps my cousin is doing it merely because she is bored." Alexander suspected boredom was why Elaina flirted so outrageously with his friend, something he intended to put a stop to as soon as possible.

Miss Rochelle rose, her chin held high. "My cousin is not involved in smuggling. Ask her if you doubt my word." She brushed past him and exited the parlor.

Alexander stood in contemplation for a moment. He'd thought his worries about finding a smuggler in his household were over. Now it appeared he was wrong. Or perhaps it was Waite who was wrong. Was it possible someone else was merely using his land and no one at the Chase was involved? He hoped that would be the case, but he would find out the truth. It seemed he and Sir Roger were going to have to stand watch once again to find who was using Landry Chase lands to run illegal goods.

Having arrived at that unfortunate conclusion, his lordship strode out of the parlor. He stepped into the sunshine in front of the inn to discover his cousin returned, not the least repentant for having abandoned them on the docks.

"I had a personal matter to handle, cousin." Elaina's tone was defiant. "I am perfectly capable of handling an errand on my own."

We'd Like to Invite You to Subscribe to Zebra's Regency Romance Book Club and Give You a Gift of 4 Free Books as Your Introduction! (Worth $19.96!)

If you're a Regency lover, imagine the joy of getting 4 FREE Zebra Regency Romances and then the chance to have these lovely stories delivered to your home each month at the lowest price available! Well, that's our offer to you and here's how you benefit by becoming a Regency Romance subscriber:

- 4 FREE Introductory Regency Romances are delivered to your doorstep
- 4 BRAND NEW Regencies are then delivered each month (usually before they're available in bookstores)
- Subscribers save almost $4.00 every month
- Home delivery is always FREE
- You also receive a FREE monthly newsletter, which features author profiles, discounts, subscriber benefits, book previews and more
- No risks or obligations...in other words, you can cancel whenever you wish with no questions asked

Join the thousands of readers who enjoy the savings and convenience offered to Regency Romance subscribers. After your initial introductory shipment, you receive 4 brand-new Zebra Regency Romances each month to examine for 10 days. Then, if you decide to keep the books, you'll pay the preferred subscriber's price of just $4.00 per title. That's only $16.00 for all 4 books and there's never an extra charge for shipping and handling.

It's a no-lose proposition, so return the FREE BOOK CERTIFICATE today!

Say Yes to 4 Free Books!
Complete and return the order card to receive this
$19.96 value, ABSOLUTELY FREE!

If the certificate is missing below, write to:
Regency Romance Book Club
P.O. Box 5214, Clifton, New Jersey 07015-5214
or call TOLL-FREE 1-888-345-BOOK
Visit our website at www.kensingtonbooks.com.

FREE BOOK CERTIFICATE

YES! Please rush me 4 Zebra Regency Romances without cost or obligation. I understand that each month thereafter I will be able to preview 4 brand-new Regency Romances FREE for 10 days. Then, if I should decide to keep them, I will pay the money-saving preferred subscriber's price of just $16.00 for all 4...that's a savings of almost $4 off the publisher's price with no additional charge for shipping and handling. I may return any shipment within 10 days and owe nothing, and I may cancel this subscription at any time. My 4 FREE books will be mine to keep in any case.

Name _____

Address _____ Apt. _____

City _____ State _____ Zip _____

Telephone ( ) _____

Signature _____ RN041A
(If under 18, parent or guardian must sign.)

llı..lıl....llllı...lll.l.lıl.l.l.l..l.l.l.l..llıl..l

REGENCY ROMANCE BOOK CLUB
Zebra Home Subscription Service, Inc.
P.O. Box 5214
Clifton NJ 07015-5214

PLACE
STAMP
HERE

Clearly this young lady was used to doing as she pleased. Alexander stepped forward and took her arm, marching her to the carriage. "Of late I have heard rumors of some of your earlier escapades. You are far too old to be engaging in such foolishness. Know that I shall be watching you very closely. I must inform you and Miss Rochelle that from this time hence, you are not to set foot out of the Chase without a proper escort now that we have sufficient maids and footmen."

A horrified look passed between the young ladies, but the baron could have no idea of the true nature of his edict. He'd inadvertently doomed Miss Rochelle to a nocturnal visit to the mill.

The carriage ride back to Landry Chase was accomplished in heavy silence. Both young ladies sat with hands folded, staring out either window. No sooner were the stairs let down than the young ladies disappeared into the Chase. By the time the gentlemen entered the Great Hall, the ladies had gone upstairs where they would stay for much of the remainder of the day.

As the gentlemen settled in the library, Sir Roger quirked one brow at his friend. "What has happened to put you all in a fume? I know it was a bit improper for Miss Addington to be going about without a—"

Alexander waved a hand. "It's not that. There is far worse." He recounted the meeting with Captain Waite and the man's accusations about Elaina. "Miss Rochelle staunchly defended her cousin, but—"

"Miss Addington a smuggler? Balderdash!" Sir Roger showed not the least doubt in the young lady's innocence.

"There are certain things about my cousin of which you are unaware." Alexander wondered if his friend's attraction to the young lady was blinding him to her true nature. "She has been in numerous minor scandals which appear to be common knowledge in the neighborhood."

"Childish pranks, perhaps, but I won't believe her a smuggler, my friend. And to prove it I will join you on watch again tonight." With that, Sir Roger exited the library. Alexander hoped the baronet was right. All he knew for certain was it was going to be a long night.

Upstairs, the ladies sat on the bed in Miss Addington's room looking at the money Elaina had poured from her reticule onto the counterpane. She scooped up a handful of coins, then let them fall back through her fingers to the bed. "Do you think this will be sufficient for the Frenchman?"

Valara nodded her head as she fingered a farthing. "The small denomination will make the money seem more than it truly is in the dark."

"When will you take it to the mill?"

"Not yet. I wouldn't want someone to come along and accidently find the hiding place and abscond with the money. I won't go tonight to alleviate some of the suspicion on his lordship's part." Valara gathered the coins and put them in her own reticule.

Elaina slid off the bed. "What got Cousin Alexander's nose out of joint?"

Valara quickly told of Captain Waite's accusation and recounting of Elaina's escapade with Mr. Akers's pigeons.

"Waite! Why that underbred little upstart! He has run about unable to catch a single smuggler." Elaina's face grew pink and she began to pace about on the worn carpeting. "Why, I've a good mind to play a very nasty—"

"Elaina!" Valara rose and went to her cousin. "You cannot do anything that will bring attention to us at the Chase. Especially not now."

Miss Addington blushed and hung her head. "I quite forgot that we truly do have a connection to the smugglers, albeit not for personal gain."

A knock sounded at the door. The new upstairs maid entered to inform Miss Addington that her mother was asking for her and Miss Rochelle.

"Tell Lady Landry we will be there in a moment." Valara smiled at the maid. As the door closed behind the servant, she turned back to her cousin. "We must go about our normal activities for the next two days. I feel certain Lord Landry and Sir Roger are going to be watching the comings and goings at the manor very closely. We don't want to arouse any suspicion."

Elaina nodded her agreement, then frowned. "How are you going to slip away to put the money in the mill if Alexander is watching?"

"I don't know, but I will think of something." With that, the young ladies made their way to the dowager baroness's room, where they faced a barrage of questions about the new baron and his activities.

Later, as Elaina read to her mother, Valara sat sewing the shirts for the orphanage. She thought it fortunate that Aunt Belinda was so distracted by her aches, pains, and complaints, as usual, that she paid little attention to what her daughter and niece were about.

The following afternoon, Valara stood in the front hall drawing on her gloves, preparing to depart for her biweekly visit to Seaforth Orphanage, when her brother came strolling down the stairs. "Going to visit Old Binny and his boys?"

"I always go on Wednesdays, and you shouldn't speak of the reverend so disrespectfully. He is a good man."

Neville shrugged. "Good, but a bit single-minded when it comes to the orphanage. I hope you won't ever consider marrying him, for you must know you would always be second to Seaforth in his mind."

"Marry Mr. Binion!" Valara's eyes widened in shock. "Why, the thought never crossed my mind." She had always veered away from thoughts of her own home and family. She'd known from the time of her father's death that penniless young females didn't marry and have children, they cared for other people's. Her aunt had spared her that fate, at least for the present, but she wasn't such a fool that she didn't realize what awaited her in the years to come unless her circumstances changed. Then a vision of Mr. Binion's tall, gaunt frame, pasty skin, and sparse brown hair came to mind and she shuddered. With an effort, she reminded herself he *was* a good man—despite his marked resemblance to a corpse.

Neville, oblivious to his sister's thoughts, added, "Well, you must marry someone, and he certainly seems enraptured with your interest in the orphanage, a subject near and dear to his heart."

"Don't be ridiculous, Neville. You and I cannot be thinking of such things until your future is more certain. Have you spoken with Lord Landry about school?" She picked up the package of shirts she'd sewn. Unbidden, the image of the baron replaced that of the reverend in her thoughts. Her heartbeat seemed to grow more rapid as her mind lingered enjoyably on his dark looks.

"I told him I want to go to Naval College. I quite like the sea, and one can earn a decent income." Neville grew thoughtful a moment, then lowered his voice. "Speaking of his lordship, did you know Alexander and Sir Roger were out in the woods again last night looking for smugglers? Saw 'em from my window. It puzzles me, since he knows I am not involved and have promised not to be out at night."

Valara fingered the string on the package, knowing full well whom the gentlemen were expecting, but she averted her gaze from her brother. "No doubt he has his reasons for being out at night. I must go or I shall be late for my lessons." She bid her brother good day and crossed the hall ready to depart the Chase, but Bainbridge stepped into her path as she neared the door.

"Now, Miss Valara, you aren't thinking of leaving without a proper escort?" The butler's face puckered into a frown.

"Good heavens, Bainbridge, I have been walking to the orphanage alone these many months without a footman or maid, and I see no reason to do otherwise."

The old family retainer shook his head and signaled one of the new footmen. "Things have changed here at the Chase, miss. His lordship has given orders that the young ladies of the house cannot be wandering about the neighborhood unaccompanied."

Valara was about to protest. Then she remembered Lord Landry's edict of the previous day. With a sigh she said, "Very well." She managed a smile for the approaching young footman, since he wasn't at fault for the situation. "What is your name?"

"Luther, miss." The young man, scarcely as old as Neville, looked rather incongruous in his gray wig.

"Well, Luther, we have rather a long walk ahead of us." The young lady exited the manor, the new servant on her heels.

As she walked down the drive, her thoughts turned to how she might manage to take the money to the mill, especially now that she wouldn't be allowed to leave the manor without a footman or maid in attendance. There was also the problem of his lordship's nightly searches. She would have to devise some kind of diversion to keep the gentlemen occupied so she could slip away. What that diversion might be, she didn't have any idea as yet.

She would talk the matter over with her cousin. Elaina

had far more experience in these covert matters than she.

Just then she heard the sound of a carriage behind her and moved to the side of the road.

A curricle drawn by a set of matched grays drew to a halt beside her, and she looked up into Lord Landry's face, which held a tentative smile. "Have you forgiven me enough for my wild accusations about my cousin to accept a ride, Miss Rochelle?"

Valara tilted her head. "Do you still think Ellie involved with smugglers, my lord?"

"Let us say that after last night I am more convinced it is a figment of Captain Waite's imagination than I was. I believe it is more likely my lands are being made use of by the Gentlemen and that has persuaded the Riding Officer that someone at the Chase is involved."

While that didn't leave Elaina guilt free in the Gentleman's view, it was likely all Valara could expect at present without implicating herself. "I shall gladly accept a ride if you are going toward the village."

"I have no set destination. I am merely testing this pair of grays that the steward found for me yesterday in Holt to see how they manage as a team. I am at your service." Lord Landry stood with his foot braced against the splashboard and helped her into the carriage as he urged the footman to jump up behind.

"Then I am for Seaforth Orphanage. It is on the far side of Cley." She settled beside the gentleman and set her gaze straight ahead, trying not to allow his nearness to unnerve her. She told herself it was because of her guilty secret, but when his arm brushed hers as he drove his team, she experienced a breathlessness that was not entirely unpleasant.

Unaware of his effect on her, the gentleman inquired, "Your brother mentioned the orphanage earlier. Is Seaforth one of Lord Westoke's charities?"

Struggling to gather her wits, Valara gave a mirthless laugh. "Hardly, my lord. If the earl has any charitable ventures, we are unaware of them here in Norfolk. Seaforth Manor was left to Mr. Binion by a particularly generous lady with the stipulation it be used as an orphanage. Unfortunately, she had more goodness of heart than fortune, and it has been left to the reverend to find the funds. He keeps it running due only to the generosity of the local parishes that donate what they can, which in hard times can be little. But he has been sensible and keeps the boys until they are eighteen. They do much of the upkeep and keep things running smoothly for the younger ones. Some even take jobs to help out. Unfortunately, he has to keep the number of boys in residence low for that reason."

His lordship nodded, then concentrated on his driving as they approached the turn to Cley. Valara directed him to keep to the left, and they were soon past the small village. Within minutes they turned inland into small woods. After more than a mile, an old stone manor set in a small park came into view. Young men could be seen working a large vegetable garden at the side of the manor as far younger ones frolicked about near an old maze.

"This is an excellent location for an orphanage. Your Mr. Binion appears to be managing nicely. Still, what a place this size needs is a benefactor. If you would like, I know several people who have an interest in charities, and I could write to them."

"That would be wonderful." As the carriage drew to a halt, Valara hesitated a moment then asked, "Would you care for a tour of the place?"

Eying the aging building, he smiled. "I should like that, Miss Rochelle. It will allow me to make note of what is needed."

While they waited for the footman to go to his lordship's team, a burly young man stepped from the tree he was trimming. "Good morning, Miss Rochelle."

Valara smiled. "Good morning, Danny. Is the reverend here today? I have brought someone to meet him."

"I'll fetch him." The young man hurried into the building as Valara and the baron stepped down from the carriage.

"Danny is one of Mr. Binion's best helpers, but I have been hoping he might find a paying job in Holt."

Landry smiled down at her. "Perhaps Mr. Bailey could find a position for him in the stables at the Chase."

"Oh, no!" Valara blushed. "That is very kind of you, but Danny knows how to read and write. Do you think you might find a position for him where he could use such skills?" She looked hopeful.

"Not I, but Sir Roger's grandfather is always looking for clerks. I shall speak to him about the boy."

She placed a hand on his arm in her gratitude. "Thank you, sir. You cannot know what it will mean to the other boys to know one of their own has done well."

The doors of the manor opened and a scowling Mr. Binion hurried forward. There could be little doubt that the reverend was not well pleased to see his lovely tutor smiling up at a handsome gentleman.

"Good day, Miss Rochelle. The boys have been eagerly awaiting you in the schoolroom." He glared at the stranger, which only made his gaunt face look more cadaverous than before.

Valara quickly made the introductions, but the clergyman's eyes only narrowed more with the news he was meeting the new Baron Landry.

"I have heard much of you from her ladyship over the years. A *soldier*, if memory serves me." Binion said the word as if it were some plague.

Lord Landry merely quirked a brow in wry amusement. "Considering that I only met my esteemed aunt a few days ago, I doubt Lady Landry knows much about me or my military career."

Well knowing what her aunt's opinion was and in a rush to keep Mr. Binion from saying anything rash based on her ladyship's prejudiced view, Valara said, "His lordship would like to look over the orphanage, sir. He thinks he might be able to help us find a benefactor from among his friends."

"You are too kind, my lord." The reverend said the words with a smile that didn't reach his eyes, his rigid stance showing he doubted the baron would or could do any such thing. "I had not known there were quite so many wealthy soldiers in the ranks that you might call upon, my lord."

To Valara's relief, the baron surprisingly took no offense. He laughed, then surveyed the orphanage with the eye of someone used to organizing matters. "We were a mixed lot, Mr. Binion, but I was thinking of calling on some of my other friends."

She couldn't understand what had the clergyman behaving in such an odd manner. The orphanage was his passion, yet here he was about to whistle away a prospect for financial security. Had her aunt so thoroughly blackened Lord Landry's character?

She debated a moment about whether she should go to the waiting children or help show the baron round the manor and keep Mr. Binion from insulting a man who had merely offered to help. Perhaps all the clergyman needed was some time to see Lady Landry's slander was just that. "I shall go and begin my class," she said. "Perhaps you would show his lordship what Seaforth needs."

The young lady departed, leaving behind two gentlemen who stood in uncomfortable silence. The gaunt young clergyman eyed the baron with mixed emotions. He was torn between his devotion to the boys in the orphanage and his firm belief that all his good works had been rewarded with the arrival of the beautiful Miss Valara Rochelle. Only his current circumstances had made him hold his tongue. He'd been eagerly awaiting the return of Lord Westoke, knowing that the earl owned the living here in Cley where the parson was about to retire. With that appointment, Arlon Binion would be able to take a bride, and Miss Rochelle was the lady he'd chosen.

At last the reverend tamped down his jealousy of the young lord, hoping that the gentleman was truthful in his desire to help Seaforth and not merely attempting to impress Valara. He ushered the gentleman into the main hall with a bit more enthusiasm. "This way, my lord. I will show you the manor."

The clergyman led Lord Landry about Seaforth, making certain to avoid the room where Miss Rochelle was instructing the boys. The baron asked intelligent questions about their current needs and what the building's full capacity could be if money weren't an issue. The vicar was soon full of enthusiasm as he explained all the possibilities.

As they inspected the rooms where the residents slept, his lordship casually inquired, "Have you known Miss Rochelle long, Mr. Binion?"

"For all the years she has lived in Cley, my lord. But she has only been teaching the boys since last summer." The man stiffened at the question about the young lady. All his earlier animosity returned as he eyed the baron closely. With an inspired thought, he announced, "She is devoted to the orphanage and . . . perhaps I should tell you there is something of an understanding between us."

In truth, there was, but not the kind that meant marriage. On her first day last summer, the lady had promised to do all in her power to teach all his young lads to read before they went out into the world.

A slight frown traveled over the baron's face and he looked back at the young vicar questioningly, but Binion offered no further explanation. "This way, my lord."

The tour soon ended in the kitchens, where Lord Landry was introduced to Mrs. Walker, the orphanage's cook. To Mr. Binion's dismay, the woman greeted the baron with excessive civility. The plump woman with rosy cheeks bobbed a curtsy, then inquired, "My lord, I was just preparin' tea for when Miss Rochelle finished her class. She always enjoys a little refreshment before she returns to Landry Chase. Would you care to join the young lady and Mr. Binion?"

"I should be delighted, Mrs. Walker. That way I shall be able to escort Miss Rochelle back to the Chase."

The young clergyman was beside himself. How dare this man try to insinuate himself into a routine Binion had come to look forward to each week? He had come to rely on Valara Rochelle's good sense and advice about the orphanage. Determined to find at least some time alone with the young lady, he hurried to the door. "Show his lordship to the parlor, and I shall return with our Miss Rochelle as soon as she is finished."

With that, the clergyman hurried to the old schoolroom at the top of the house. He paced in front of the closed door, listening to the murmuring of the lady's voice, anxious to have a few moments to warn her about penniless adventurers. Now that he'd seen the man for himself, he was convinced her ladyship was right.

The door opened and a stream of small boys came pouring out. He ordered them outside in an unusually sharp tone. Promising himself to make amends to them later, he stepped into the room, where Valara was putting away slate tablets.

"Mr. Binion, whatever are you doing here?" She

peered eagerly over his shoulder. "Is his lordship still here?"

"He awaits us in the blue parlor. Cook has prepared refreshments, but I wanted to have a few moments alone before we joined him. I am concerned that you allowed him to bring you here. I would give you warning."

"Warning?" The young lady's brow crinkled a bit.

The reverend stepped forward and grasped her hand. Her eyes widened, and he nervously released her, allowing her to step away. "I apologize for my forwardness, my dear, but you are such an innocent I felt it my duty to warn you about gentlemen like Lord Landry."

"What do you mean, sir?" Her voice was neutral, but her beautiful blue eyes had grown cool.

"Why, it has been known in Cley for years that Mr. Hugh Addington was an adventurer and a gambler who abandoned his family and his country for his own purposes. Now his son, whose character is reputed little better, has inherited and come to see what he can plunder from the estate. You must guard your reputation closely and not be led astray by such a man. Do not be fooled by his good looks and charm, as most young girls would be. He might trifle with a beautiful girl's affections, but he is a gentleman who has little choice but to marry for money."

Valara's cheeks grew pink as her indignation rose. "Mr. Binion, you wrongly accuse his lordship. His interest is in repairing the estate, not trifling with females, as you put it. You would be well advised not to take everything my aunt has said about his lordship as the truth. She knows little more of him than the rest of the neighborhood. He has spent his life defending King and country. For that alone you should respect him. As to the other, I am not some foolish girl to fall under the spell of the first handsome man who crosses my path. Besides I shall not marry until my brother is safely settled into his own life."

"Not marry! Miss Rochelle you cannot mean—"

"I mean what I say, sir. I must take care of my brother."

Completely unaware of how her final announcement had crushed the young clergyman, Valara marched out of the schoolroom to make her way to the parlor. As she hurried down the stairs, Mr. Binion's words rang in her mind. Lord Landry might be kind to her, but in truth he likely would marry for wealth. She would be a fool to allow herself to fall in love with a man who must think of Landry Chase first. She couldn't blame him, but that didn't ease the strange pang in her chest.

For the next thirty minutes, she endured tea with a morose Mr. Binion and Lord Landry, who continued to question the vicar about the orphanage and got monosyllabic answers for his efforts. At last she announced it was time to return to Landry Chase and bid the clergyman good day. She was thankful his lordship seemed to sense her dark mood and kept the conversation light as they drove back home.

As they neared the gates of the estate, Valara realized she must contain her growing attraction to the baron. With a determined effort, she turned her thoughts to a matter that was most pressing—the Frenchman Dubois. Perhaps she would try to take the money to the mill tonight. She could slip away while Elaina entertained the gentlemen in the drawing room. She felt certain her cousin would agree with the plan.

"Are you quite well, Miss Rochelle?" His lordship asked, looking down at her with concern. "You have been rather quiet."

Valara nodded, thinking to begin her plan at once. "I am just a bit tired. I think I shall retire early this evening."

Seven

Alexander reined his team to a sedate trot as he made the turn into the gates of the Chase. He suspected his companion was more than tired. Had she and that sour vicar at the orphanage had words? And about what? Then Binion's boast about having an understanding with Miss Rochelle returned. Strange, Alex had seen nothing on the young lady's part to suggest such an attachment. Or was he merely fooling himself because he found her so appealing?

"Oh, my!" the young lady uttered, startling the baron from his musings.

Standing in front of the mansion was a black traveling carriage which would scarcely awe anyone, but behind the ancient vehicle stood four large foragons piled with trunks, carpets, and enough furniture to fill many rooms.

As they drew closer, Alexander recognized the crest of the Earl of Wotherford and knew at once his visitor was his godmother, Lady Margaret. He gave a soft chuckle, knowing the dowager countess never did anything by half, for she was quite the most managing creature he'd ever known. He'd written to request a few bolts of cloth for making gowns for the ladies of Landry Chase, and the name of a good furniture maker. Lady

Margaret had gone ten steps further. It appeared she'd brought nearly enough to furnish most of the rooms on the lower floor.

Within a matter of minutes, he and Miss Rochelle entered the green drawing room to find a befuddled Elaina holding a bolt of white spiderweb muslin, an excited Neville perusing a box of new books, and an amused Sir Roger listening to Lady Margaret's plans for the residents of the Chase. Her ladyship's great Russian wolfhound, Boris, lay sprawled on the rug in front of the fire, looking quite content with his new surroundings. Near him stood an open trunk with bolts of colorful silks, sarcenets, and muslins inside.

Miss Addington seemed to come out of her stupor as the others entered the room. "But, Lady Margaret, we are in mourning. We cannot put off wearing black." She stepped forward and put the bolt of fabric reluctantly back into the trunk.

"Balderdash, dear girl. While your mama should keep to widow's weeds, I think there is nothing wrong with your returning to colors, since your cousins may. One had only to know Bartholomew Addington to know few would expect anyone to mourn him. But I feared you might be a bit hesitant, so I brought lilac fabric and black ribbons, which is perfectly acceptable as half mourning." The dowager reached into the case and pulled out a bolt of pale lavender muslin dotted with white flock.

"Lady Margaret," Alexander called, "I see you are up to your usual ways." He grinned at his godmother, who had done much to aid him upon his arrival in England so long ago.

The dowager's face lit at the sight of her godson. "My dear boy, you are here at last, and this must be Mr. Rochelle's lovely sister. I am delighted to make your acquaintance, my dear." Without waiting for a response from Valara, her ladyship got immediately to the crux of the matter. "I have just been telling these foolish children 'tis time to move forward. A new day has dawned at Landry Chase, and there is much to do."

"I quite agree, but must it all be done in one day?" Alexander began to wonder about the wisdom of having written to his godmother to ask a small favor.

Her ladyship's mouth pursed, but there was a twinkle in her gray eyes. "At my age there is no time for dawdling, my boy. I suggest this dreadfully furnished room be emptied at once to make room for all I have brought. I have managed to come all the way from London without a single drop of rain, and I don't want all my efforts to be in vain."

Alexander came and kissed the lady's cheek. He thought her looking none the worse for wear after the journey from Town, despite her sixty-odd years. She was a tiny woman dressed in a simple blue traveling gown trimmed with black frogging. Wisps of white curls peeked from under her lacy cap. Her face was moderately lined, but nothing like one would expect from a woman of her years. "What have you been about, my lady? All I requested was a selection of material for the ladies to fashion new gowns and the name of a furniture maker."

With an airy wave of a thin hand, her ladyship turned to look about the room. "There is little that happens in London that I do not know of, Landry. It was known for years your uncle was systematically selling off all his possession to pay gaming debts. I had little doubt your new estate was sitting virtually empty." She paused and gave a thoughtful look at the green walls. "Definitely the gold settee and chairs must come in this room, unless you have an objection, dear boy."

Alexander laughed. "I shall leave all to your excellent judgment, my lady. But you must present me with a bill, for I shan't allow you to pay for filling my estate with furniture."

"Splendid!" The dowager went to the door and called for her footman. "Where have Lisette and her assistant gotten to, John? Ah, there you are, girl. Come and meet the young ladies. Miss Addington, Miss Rochelle, this is Lisette Anjou and her helper, whom you must take upstairs to the sewing room and allow to take your measurements. Mademoiselle Anjou is magical with a needle, my dears." Looking at the French seamstress, she inquired, "Did you bring the fashion plates, Lisette?"

"*Oui*, milady, zay are in zee trunk."

Lady Margaret beamed at the dazed young ladies. "You may select whatever styles you like."

Elaina frowned as two footmen came and lifted the trunk of material. "My lady, you are very kind, but I cannot think Mama will approve of my putting aside my black gowns. After all, it has been only a little over three months since Papa died."

"Child, don't worry about your mother. We have known one another for years. Do you think I could be Alexander's godmother and not know the rest of the Addington family? I shall smooth things with her. Just go and let Lisette work her magic."

Still Miss Addington lingered uncertainly, so Alexander remarked, "It is my wish, Cousin, that you at least go into half mourning, if you cannot bring yourself to completely return to colors. As my godmother said, it is a new day at the Chase, and I cannot like you and your cousins going about dressed in badly dyed attire." He turned to Miss Rochelle, who'd been quiet since entering the room. "Do you not think my aunt would wish you all to look your best?"

Valara nodded, then went to her cousin's side and lifted the black fabric of her own unfashionable skirts.

"These gowns are three years old and were rather dreadful even before they were dyed black. Come. I think Aunt Belinda will have no objection."

Elaina tilted her head slightly, her face showing some interest in the trunk for the first time. "Is there fabric for a riding habit, my lady?"

"Of course, child." Lady Margaret smiled. "Alexander said to buy a variety of colors and materials suited to red and blond hair, so I chose greens and browns, as well as the lilac, for you and pinks and blues for Miss Rochelle."

"Come, Ellie, let us see what is in the trunk." Valara locked her arm with her cousin's. "Thank you, Lady Margaret."

"Don't thank me, child. I was merely following Alexander's orders." The lady smiled at her godson.

After thanking the baron, the young ladies departed with the seamstress. Before Alexander could get a word in edgewise, however, Lady Margaret once again took control of matters. She soon had half the Chase's footmen busy unloading furniture while the other half emptied the drawing room.

It wasn't till later in the afternoon when Alexander had a moment to himself that he suddenly wondered what Miss Rochelle would look like in a fashionable new gown, her lovely hair curled about her face. Then he reminded himself that, according to Mr. Binion, the young lady was spoken for.

Lisette dropped the measuring tape and wrote the final measurements for Valara on a slip paper. *"Voila, mademoiselle,* zat es all I need. With a bit of luck, you each shall have zee new evening gown by tomorrow night."

In French, Valara said, "Thank you, Lisette, but do

not overtire yourself or Cecily. We are not expecting to entertain or be entertained any time soon."

"Mademoiselle, your French is flawless." Lisette said, keeping to her native tongue.

Valara explained she and her brother were half French. For the next several moments they discussed Paris, the seamstress wishing to return and the young lady desiring to visit.

Elaina grew impatient, unable to follow the rapid flow of a language she barely understood. "Is that all you needed us for, Lisette?"

The little seamstress nodded, returning to English as she directed a question to Miss Addington. "Shall I use zee lilac, mademoiselle, or zee sea-foam green?"

Elaina ran her hand over the patterned green silk shot through with gold thread which was spread out on the table, then shook her head. "I had best stay with the lilac for now, Lisette. But definitely the golden brown wool for my new riding habit."

"Zee habit comes after zee evening gowns." Lisette wagged her finger at the young lady, but smiled. "And for you, Mademoiselle Rochelle?"

"The rose pink." Valara gestured to a pale glacé silk that reflected deeper shades of rose.

Those decisions made, the young ladies departed, leaving the seamstresses to their work. No sooner had the door closed than Valara said, "Come to my room. I wish to speak with you."

Once safely behind the thick oak door of her bedchamber, she turned to her cousin. "I have decided tonight is perfect to go to the mill, what with you and now Lady Margaret to distract Lord Landry and Sir Roger. I shall claim fatigue shortly after we dine, then slip out the back. I can make it to the mill and back in less than an hour."

Elaina's eyes widened. "Are you certain?"

"It is the perfect time. Lord Landry and his godmother will have much news to impart to one another. He will take little note of my retiring early."

"I wish I could go with you," She remarked wistfully. Then, as her cousin shook her head, Elaina sighed. "I promise to make certain everyone is distracted."

Later, as she dressed for dinner, Valara hoped that all would go smoothly. She walked to the window and drew back the curtains. The darkening sky was clear and the wind had fallen. She shouldn't have the least trouble making it to the mill and back without discovery.

At least she prayed she wouldn't.

" 'Tis sad but true that Lady Landry is as much a henwit now as in her youth," Lady Margaret announced to her godson as they strolled along in the darkness on the terrace that evening.

Alexander made no comment on his aunt's character despite thoroughly agreeing with her ladyship. "Your meeting this afternoon did not go well, then."

"Well enough, for I got her to agree to new gowns for the young ladies, but Belinda Addington has this absurd notion you won't stay long in Norfolk."

Alexander chuckled softly. "I am well aware of her wish for me to be gone, and preferably to Hades, unless I miss my guess. She doesn't realize I am not my father or my uncle."

Just then Miss Rochelle appeared in the doorway of the drawing room, her golden hair forming the illusion of a halo from the light in the drawing room behind her. "I wish to bid you good night, Lady Margaret, Lord Landry. I am a bit tired after my visit to the orphanage this morning."

Alexander was suddenly reminded of the young boy's calling her an angel at the quay. As her ladyship bid the young lady to have a pleasant sleep, he realized Miss Rochelle had been the only person not to have caused him trouble, and in that sense she *was* an angel. Coming out of his bemusement, he bid the young lady good night. After she departed and they'd resumed their strolling, Lady Margaret observed, "A very remarkable young woman, unless I miss my guess. Bainbridge was singing her praises this afternoon."

"Have you been gossiping with the servants, Godmother?" Alex teased, mostly to keep his thoughts about Valara to himself.

"Of course, my boy. How else will I know what has been happening at the Chase?"

He shook his head in amazement that she openly admitted to such a social offense. "You are an original, madam. And what have you learned about us?"

The dowager halted and looked him square in the face. "Nothing of any great import. The worst I heard was of your cousin's exploits, but of late even she has behaved herself, hoping for Westoke to come up to scratch." She paused, then added, "But unless he hurries, I fear your friend, Sir Roger, might steal a march on him. There is a look in his eyes when he speaks to Elaina—"

"As if Lady Landry would even consider an offer from Roger, knowing his lineage."

A chuckle rumbled deep within the dowager's chest. "But she hasn't reckoned with me, and I quite like Sir Roger. As to Miss Rochelle, she has been fulfilling Lady Landry's duties here for years. She would make an excellent wife." Her ladyship arched a brow and grinned up at him.

"Lady Margaret, don't start matchmaking your very first night at Landry Chase. I won't have my friend set up for such a disappointment. As for myself, I have too much on my plate just now to be thinking of a bride."

Especially one who might already have given her heart to the vicar.

"I make no promises, dear boy. But I shall do nothing for the moment. Will you show me the estate in the morning? I should like to see the place once again."

Glad the lady had moved on to other matters, he replied, "I fear you will be appalled at the state of disrepair to which it has fallen, but I have the steward working nonstop to set matters to rights. What time would you like your tour?"

They set the time for ten the following morning. Then her ladyship announced her journey had left her quite fatigued as well, and she, too, would retire. "Escort me to my rooms, and I shall allow you to read the letter I received from the newlyweds in Italy just before I departed London."

Passing through the drawing room, Alexander informed the others that Lady Margaret was retiring.

Elaina bounced to her feet from the new spinet's bench. "You will return to listen to me play, won't you, Cousin?"

He was surprised at her eagerness for him to return, especially after their contretemps the previous afternoon. "I shall be able to hear you from the library if I leave both doors open. I fear I have some documents to read that Mr. Bailey left just before we dined. Do continue to entertain us."

The young lady sat down and, after a moment's hesitation, returned to the piece she'd been playing. Alexander escorted Lady Margaret to her rooms, where he read the short note from his eldest sister. He was pleased to see they intended to return to England by the end of April. He hoped the Chase would be ready to receive visitors by then, but no matter. All he wanted was to see Adriana and meet the man who'd captured her heart.

He bid her ladyship good night, then stepped into

the hall. He headed back down the stairs, the sounds of the spinet echoing through the hall. As he reached the library door, a strange restlessness overtook him. He'd been a man used to the outdoor life of a soldier, and suddenly his every waking moment seemed to be spent going over estate matters. Without a glance at the papers piled on his desk, he strode through the room and out the library door, which opened onto the east lawn.

It took several moments for Alexander's eyes to adjust to the all-consuming darkness of the moonless night. At last the forms of trees and shrubs began to take shape. It was scarcely nine o'clock, but night was in full bloom. He suddenly wondered if he and Sir Roger had been starting their vigilance for the smugglers too late in the evening.

On impulse, he crossed the lawn, heading straight for the trees where he knew a path led to the mill. There could be little doubt the slate tower played some role in the local smuggling.

He was halfway along the wooded path when a pistol shot echoed through the trees. Fear gripped him as he raced toward the mill, whence the gunfire seemed to have come. He'd seen plenty of death and destruction on the battlefield, but he wasn't prepared to find it here in the quiet countryside of Norfolk.

As he exited the trees, he could see the silhouettes of a group of men clustered together near the mill tower. Were they dragoons or smugglers? A babble of excited voices assailed him, but he couldn't make out what was being said.

He suddenly wished he'd brought his pistol. Still he forged ahead, determined to find out who had fired a shot on his property and who had been the target.

As the baron neared the group, Waite's voice shouted

out, "We've got you now, my boy. There is no need to resist further. Taylor, the lantern."

Someone unshuttered a lantern, and the group was suddenly awash in golden light. Alexander's heart seemed to freeze for just a moment at the sight that greeted him. There in the clutches of two dragoons was Miss Valara Rochelle in a dark hooded cloak, struggling to break free, her blond curls tumbled about her shoulders.

Without the least plan, Alexander forged into the circle of light and ordered, "Unhand that woman at once."

Perhaps it was the baron's commanding tone, or merely the shock of discovering they had captured a woman, but the dragoons complied with the order, stepping back from their captive. Freed, she flew at Alexander, and he took the trembling young woman in his arms. His mind reeled at the idea that Miss Rochelle was somehow involved in smuggling, but as his gaze met Waite's over her head, Alex knew he would do all in his power to save her from herself.

With a flash of inspiration, an idea came to him to explain their being on the marshes. He crushed Valara to him, then tilted her chin and kissed her firmly on her lips. To his surprise, she kissed him back.

He was briefly aware of the dazed expression on the young lady's face as he drew back, but he had no time to think what it meant. Instead he continued with the role he'd cast himself in. "Are you unharmed, my dear?"

Even in the dim light of the lantern, he could see fear tempered with some other strong emotion in her blue eyes as she nodded. Then she melted into the comfort of his arms, pressing her head against his chest. He was strangely aware of her feminine softness and the rapid beating of her heart against his as his arms tightened round her.

Suddenly he was furious that she had been accosted on his own lands, no matter her reason for being out at night. He scowled over her head at the Riding Officer. "What is the meaning of this outrage, sir? How dare you endanger Miss Rochelle by discharging a pistol so near her? She should be able to walk about my estate without fear of being accosted by anyone."

Waite tucked his pistol into his belt, but there was no remorse or regret on his face as he stared back at his lordship and the young lady. "What were you doing out here at the mill tonight, Miss Rochelle?"

"I—I—that is—"

Alexander interrupted before she could ruin his plan. "Miss Rochelle came out to meet me, Captain Waite."

The Riding Officer sneered, "I am no flat, my lord. I have been at catching smugglers for some time. You can see this young lady any time of the day at the Chase. You shall need to spin a better yarn than that."

The baron arched one brow. "As the entire neighborhood no doubt is aware, my aunt does not approve of me. I was hoping to spare Lara her ladyship's recriminations for her involvement with me." He gently stroked her hair in a gesture that felt natural, then changed his face into a stony mask as he glared at the tidesman. "But I don't have to give you or Lady Landry any explanation for what I do on my own lands. Kindly take your men and be gone, sir. You have caused enough of a disturbance this evening, and all for naught. I should hate to have to complain to your superiors about your accosting members of my household."

The Riding Officer looked from Lord Landry to Miss Rochelle, but doubt was etched in every line on his face.

Still, the man could not disprove what the baron was saying, and he was not such a fool as to forget that the Customs Board might well take the word of a gentleman over his any day. A great struggle took place in his mind, but at last he found the words to protect his position. "I do regret if we frightened you, Miss Rochelle. As you know, this beach is often used by smugglers, and we mistook you for one. Mayhap you should find some other place to tryst"—he couldn't resist sneering as he said the word—"with his lordship than on the marshes, where it ain't safe."

The man's every word indicated he thought the story a hum, but Alexander made no further comment. He merely glared back at the Riding Officer until Waite called for his men to assemble.

The baron waited until the captain and his men moved off down the beach before he released his hold on Miss Rochelle. Once again in overwhelming darkness, he couldn't see her features as he asked, "Have you taken leave of your senses? You could have been shot by that overzealous fool. What the devil are you doing out here?"

"I-it is not what you think, my lord." Her voice was barely above a whisper.

"Miss Rochelle, I have just played the besotted lover for Captain Waite. Don't you think I deserve the truth?"

"It is not my secret alone to tell, my lord. You took Neville's word when he told you he was not smuggling, and I hope you will take mine as well."

Alexander was torn. He wanted the truth, but she was right. He *had* taken young Rochelle's word on faith, and it had proven true. Yet this was a far more damning situation. Finally, in the name of fairness, he spoke through stiff lips. "Very well. I shall not press you, but I hope you will never again risk your safety in such a foolish manner."

The young lady was silent a moment. "I am no fool, my lord."

Alexander nodded, then said, "Shall we return to the Chase?"

They walked back through the woods in silence, but Alexander's thoughts raced from one possibility to another as to why Valara had been at the mill. Neville had gone out to meet a woman. Had Miss Rochelle gone to meet a man?

There was a strange tightening in his chest at the thought, but he knew little about this young woman other than she stirred his blood in some way. Had her trip to the marshes been to meet a lover? Was there someone her aunt had so disapproved of that Miss Rochelle had been forced to meet him secretly? Surely Mr. Binion did not fit that description, nor could he see the need for such meetings. She saw him regularly at the orphanage.

If it was a lovers' rendezvous, it was with someone else. Then he remembered something Neville had said during their ride to the mill. There was a neighbor Aunt Belinda disliked and thought a mushroom. What had his name been? Akers. Mr. Ronald Akers.

Alex suddenly thought it strange he could dislike someone he'd never met. But then, he might be rushing to false conclusions. She hadn't said she'd been meeting someone, only that she was not smuggling. Yet as he turned the possibilities over in his mind, nothing but a tryst seemed to explain why a beautiful young woman would be out at night.

On reaching the Chase, the pair entered through the side door to the library. He knew a desire to keep the lady with him, to insist she explain fully why she had been on the marshes. As she crossed the room, he called, "Miss Rochelle."

She halted at the door, her blue gaze wary as she

tugged at the ribbon that held her cloak in place. "My lord?"

Mesmerized, Alexander watched the velvet fabric slide from her shoulders and reveal the soft white skin rising and falling above her bodice. His loins stirred at so simple an act as removing a cloak, and he admitted to himself he wanted Valara Rochelle. He gripped the edge of his desk, reminding himself this woman had secrets. "I won't press you to tell what you cannot, only I beg of you to have a care. The marshes are dangerous, especially at night." His gaze locked with hers, and time seemed to halt.

At last the young lady sighed. "I promise I will explain when I am able."

Valara Rochelle departed, leaving Alexander needing a drink badly. After pouring himself a generous portion in a glass, he realized he was more perplexed than ever about what was going on in the marshes at night, about what he could do about it, and about his growing desire for the enigmatic beauty.

Valara closed the door to her bedchamber and leaned against the wood. Her mind was still in a whirl about the shocking events earlier. Capture—and then salvation at the hands of Lord Landry. The kiss.

She lifted her fingers to her lips and traced the outline of where his mouth had caressed hers. For just that brief moment, it had driven everything from her head. But then, after all had calmed down, he'd wanted the truth, and she had been unable to betray her uncle's confidence.

Her hand fell from her lips. She mustn't put too much stock in his actions tonight. His lordship had kissed her to save her from the gaol, nothing more. With a disappointed sigh, she moved across the room to her desk. She lifted her skirt and took the wrapped cloth packet of money from a pocket in her underskirt where she'd hidden it. All that and she hadn't gotten a chance to put the money in the box. She put the packet in a drawer, then went to the window to look out into the darkness.

She would have to try to go back to the mill sometime within the next three days or nights. There could be little doubt his lordship would be even more vigilant after tonight's debacle, but her uncle's mission—nay, even his life—might depend on her.

Eight

By noon the following day, much of Cley and the neighboring families had heard of the encounter Lord Landry and Miss Rochelle had with the Riding Officer on the marshes. Speculation was rampant that his lordship's flaw wasn't gambling, like his father and uncle, but trifling with women. Reason told all the gossips that a half-pay soldier would have to marry for money and that the penniless Miss Rochelle was a mere fling while he attempted to put the estate back to a more profitable state.

Unaware of the latest gossip, one gentleman in the neighborhood had taken a pronounced interest in the new baron's circumstances.

"The new Lord Landry has been spending a great deal of money on new servants and repairs at the Chase." In his private apartments at Westwood Manor, Simon Crane, eighth Earl of Westoke, watched as his valet fashioned his black locks into a windswept. Finally satisfied with his personal servant's efforts, the earl gestured the valet gone. He moved his head back and forth to admire the finished look in the mirror, then turned to his secretary, who hovered nearby. "What more have you learned about the man?"

Mr. Wicks pushed his glasses up on his bulbous nose

and looked down at the notes he'd made. "His steward told ours that the gentleman has settled *all* the late baron's outstanding debts, which I understand was a considerable sum. He has ordered the old mill be repaired and reopened. Workers are already renovating the Dower House. Also, there is a trip planned during the summer to Yorkshire, purportedly to buy livestock."

The earl puckered his lips thoughtfully before he remarked, "That hardly sounds like a penniless soldier. It seems Hugh's son has returned a nabob. Was he in India?"

"Not that I can learn, my lord. But I do understand he is accompanied by Sir Roger Howard, who I discovered is Thaddeus Hull's grandson. Rumor is the men were at Eton together." The secretary nodded as if that explained Lord Landry's situation.

"Who the devil is Thaddeus Hull?" Westoke could greet nearly every peer who frequented Town by name, but he hadn't a clue as to the rest of London's extensive population.

"Hull is one of the richest Cits in London, my lord. If I were to hazard a guess, I would think the baron has tied his fortunes to the old man and prospered."

The earl's eyes glittered at that news. "Write my solicitor in London. See what he can find out about this Alexander Addington."

"Very good, my lord." Mr. Wicks scribbled a note on his pad.

"Are all the arrangements ready for tomorrow night?" The earl rose and shrugged on his gray riding coat with the secretary's aid.

"Exactly as you requested, my lord."

"Excellent. Then that will be all for now." The secretary left the earl to finish his toilette.

The gentleman stared at his reflection in the mirror and a smirk settled on his handsome face before he said aloud, "Well, dear Blythe, I may well have found the gentleman to take you off my hands." With a final adjustment to his cravat, he strode from the room, calling for his mount. At Landry Chase, he intended to welcome Lord Landry to Norfolk as propriety decreed and invite him to a party at Westwood.

The Earl of Westoke was a singularly self-absorbed young man. In the normal course of things, he would have paid little attention to someone ascending to a title in the neighborhood, but circumstances with his sister changed all that. The idea of having his household in London disrupted for an entire Season with a young girl making her come out held little appeal. Worse, Blythe had manage to alienate their only living aunt by her forward conduct in Bath, and no one was willing to act as the girl's chaperon.

Westoke led life just as he wished. In Town, he indulged his love of fine wine, good food, beautiful actresses, and blood sports. It was rare that he paid the least attention to what anyone else needed or wanted. But with the arrival of his sister's eighteenth birthday, his Aunt Virginia had managed to capture his attention in a most unpleasant way. The old harridan had deposited his sister on his doorstep in London and warned that he should find her a husband with due haste before she created a scandal. Without the least thought for his feelings, the old girl had hied back to Bath, washing her hands of both her niece and her nephew.

In something of a huff, he'd set out for Norfolk on the advice of his friend Markham. The dandy had warned him there was no worse place in the world for a hoyden than London, where all and sundry could learn of her foibles. Not wanting the girl to ruin her chances for marriage, he'd set out for the family seat with a protesting Blythe in tow, determined to find a way not to allow her back to Town until she was someone else's responsibility. He'd stopped briefly at his uncle's house to invite his cousin, Miss Nora Crane, to come and act as his sister's companion. The dowdy girl had little in common with her cousin, but she had a sensible head on her shoulders, according to Aunt Virginia, and would keep Blythe from under foot and hopefully out of scandal.

On arriving at Westwood, the earl had set about at once having his secretary scour the countryside for eligible young men, and the man seemed to have done his job well. Wicks had found several prospects, but none so good as Landry. Simon would be perfectly content to marry her to a baron, especially one who appeared to be plump in the pockets.

It was past noon when Westoke mounted his latest purchase, an Arabian descended from the Godolphin line, and set out for his nearest neighbors. The day was pleasant and the ride to Landry Chase took scarcely thirty minutes. Cantering up the drive, Lord Westoke took note of the army of servants working in the gardens and knew his secretary had the right of things. Lord Landry seemed to be swimming in butter. Who cared whence it had come? Fate had dealt the earl a winning hand by sending old Bart Addington to his reward at just the right moment.

A groom took the earl's horse and that gentleman strolled to the newly stained oak doors. Every where he looked, there was evidence of money being spent freely to repair the Chase.

Then Westoke's hand froze as he was about to lift the knocker. His father and the late baron had once spoken of a marriage between himself and Miss Addington. He pushed the notion aside. That had been years ago, long before old Bart had squandered his fortune. Besides, at only nine and twenty, Westoke had no intentions of being tied down by a wife, especially a penniless one with a penchant for scandal.

With that worry put aside, the earl sounded the knocker and waited. Within minutes, the butler appeared and ushered the gentleman into the green drawing room.

News of Lord Landry's meeting with the Earl of Westoke traveled quickly among the residents of the Chase. Within some ten minutes of the peer's arrival, the stillroom door opened and Elaina peeked inside. "There you are. I was wondering where you had gotten to." She entered the room, closing the door behind her. "Have you heard the news?" She came and stood beside Valara, who was busy at the table making lavender sachets.

"I have spoken to no one but the maid since last night." Valara dusted her hands and turned to her cousin. In truth, she'd been avoiding his lordship. "What has happened?"

"Westoke has come to call," Elaina said in a choked voice.

Valara rose, taking her cousin's hands. "But I thought you were quite resigned to marrying him only a few days ago. Why so upset?"

"That was before . . ." Elaina pulled free. She picked up one of the ribbons used to tie the sachet packets and began to pull it nervously through her fingers. "I know it is my duty to marry well, but I cannot like him, Lara."

Hugging her cousin, Valara then held her at arm's length. She suspected the unfinished sentence had been, *That was before Sir Roger,* but she merely said, "I am glad you have come to your senses, *but—*"

"But Mama." The two cousins exchanged a knowing

look. Each knew Lady Landry's mind was set on Westoke, and only a peer with a larger fortune or higher rank could supplant him in that lady's mind. While Sir Roger's fortune was vast, his ties to trade would be fatal in Lady Landry's mind.

Valara bit her lip, then smiled. "We may be putting the cart in front of the horse, so to speak. His lordship might only be calling to welcome Lord Landry to the neighborhood."

Her cousin shrugged and moved to pick up a dark glass bottle with dried leaves inside. She lifted the stopper, then wrinkled her nose at the pungent odor. "No matter his reason, Mama will be full of renewed hope that all will be as she wishes. Oh, there is no point in talking about things we cannot change." Elaina recapped the bottle and put it back on the table. "How did things go last night at the mill? Did you put the money in the secret alcove?"

"No." Valara sat on the stool, her shoulders sagging, and recounted the events on the marsh, save the kiss from his lordship. That was something she wanted to keep close to her heart, to savor. Very likely it might be the only one she ever experienced.

Her cousin's eyes widened as she heard the tale. "Whatever did Landry say when you told him why you were out there?"

"I didn't tell him." Valara's gaze locked on her hands. She couldn't explain to herself exactly why she hadn't told him the truth.

Elaina frowned. "You must know he would never betray your uncle Philippe. Alexander, as much as any man in England, wouldn't want Bonaparte to return."

"I do know, but . . . well, likely he would want to take matters into his own hands, and it is *my* family and *my* responsibility." Valara glared defiantly up at her cousin.

A thoughtful expression settled on Miss Addington's

lovely countenance. Then, tossing her auburn curls, she began to pace. "Well, of all the odd turns. For years *I* have been told to be more like my proper cousin—to behave myself and not kick up my heels in protest at all this dull propriety. Now I find *you* like adventuring as much as I do and are taking far more risks than I ever did, yet everyone thinks you the model of a perfect young lady."

Valara appeared stunned for a moment to be compared with a cousin who was thought something of a hoyden. Then, a smile tipped the corner of her mouth. "I cannot deny I have enjoyed my clandestine adventures." Her brows drew together. "Well, perhaps not being caught by Waite last night, but until then it seemed I was doing something of purpose. But what am I to do if his lordship presses me about why I was out last night?"

"You needn't worry. He is too much the gentleman to ask again now that you have told him you cannot say."

Valara prayed her cousin was right.

At that moment a knock sounded on the stillroom door, and a maid stepped into the room and bobbed a curtsy. "Beggin' your pardon, Miss Addington, but you and Miss Rochelle is wanted in the green drawing room right away."

Elaina shot Valara a frightened glance, then squared her shoulders. "Come, let us see why we have been summoned."

They made their way to the drawing room hand in hand. Yet the closer they got, the more Elaina's steps seemed to drag. At last they opened the door.

To their surprise, only Lady Margaret sat in front of the fireplace. Boris sprawled on the rug, asleep.

"Come in, my dears. I have the most wonderful news." Her ladyship gestured them forward. When they stood before her, she announced, "We have been invited to a party at Westwood Manor tomorrow night. Nothing grand, mind you, only dinner and a bit of dancing afterward. I have prevailed upon your mother to allow you to attend, Miss Addington, and so what do you think of that?" The elderly lady beamed up at the two girls.

Valara blinked in surprise. "My cousin is to be allowed to dance even though still in mourning?"

Her ladyship chuckled. "Good heavens, child. Since it was Westoke doing the asking Belinda would have allowed her to dance on Bart's coffin, she's so keen for the match. You needn't worry that anyone but the highest stickler will disapprove, and should anyone say a word, I shall let them know I approve, and that will be the end of that. You both shall be allowed to dance."

"Th-that was all his lordship wanted? He made no mention of me?" Elaina didn't seem able to believe her ears.

The dowager chuckled. "That was all. He was most anxious for Alexander to attend." The lady grew thoughtful a moment, then added, "Unless I miss my guess, Westoke is hoping for a match between Landry and his sister, for he praised the chit several times during the conversation." The dowager gave a knowing grin. "Men are so obvious with their matchmaking. I believe a French poet once said the greatest fool was man."

"But, my lady," Valara said, "if you refer to Boileau, I believe he was comparing humans to other species, not man to woman."

"Never mind about that. Do go find Lisette and have the final fittings for your gowns. I want you both looking your best." Lady Margaret settled back, fully content she knew best.

As the door to the drawing room closed, Elaina turned to her cousin, a glitter of excitement in her eyes.

"Do you know what this means? The earl doesn't care a fig about me, and we are to go to Westwood without Mama. I shan't have to throw myself at his lordship. We shall be able to dine and dance without the least worry."

Valara smiled wanly at her cousin's elation, but there was no joy in her heart. Lady Blythe and Lord Landry—the thought brought a sharp pain in Valara's chest.

Later, as Elaina turned in front of the mirror while Lisette made adjustments to the new evening gown, Valara struggled to put the matter of his lordship and Blythe from her mind, reminding herself she'd known he would need to marry for money. She had a far more pressing matter on her plate. How was she to manage another trip to the mill without his lordship finding out?

Much of the following day was consumed with general preparations for that evening's entertainment. There had been final fittings of the gowns, and Lady Margaret had convinced the girls to allow her personal maid, Nancy, to wash and trim their hair.

When dressed, they had been ordered to Lady Landry's room for final approval. The baroness was full of advice on how to entice Lord Westoke, to which Elaina merely nodded her head, making no comment. Valara was admonished to keep a watchful eye on her cousin and report fully any missteps.

Once past that ordeal, the young ladies hurried to Lady Margaret's apartments. As they entered, the countess, striking in deep purple with matching turban, turned from the fireplace and stood speechless for a moment. She soon announced that the little French seamstress and Nancy had outdone themselves. Elaina was resplendent in the lavender with white dot that possessed tiny puffed sleeves and a deep flounce. Her auburn curls were entwined with lavender and white ribbons. Valara's high-waisted pink gown had a white spiderweb muslin overskirt that opened in the front. The maid had fashioned the girl's blond hair in the Grecian style and had nestled small pink roses among the curls.

"My dears, you are both diamonds of the first water. I should be proud to act as your chaperon in London, should you decide to come. You are perfect save for a little jewelry. Nancy, my case."

"Oh, Lady Margaret you mustn't." Valara shook her head. She was certain she'd never looked so fine, thanks to the dowager's efforts, and she didn't think it proper to allow the lady, a virtual stranger a few days ago, to do more.

"Nonsense, child. We must have you looking your best." Her ladyship chose an amethyst teardrop necklace and matching ear bobs for Elaina, and pronounced that only pearls would suit Valara's pink gown.

As the ladies put the final touches on their toilette, the baron and his friend were in the drawing room, awaiting the arrival of the rest of the members of the household. Alexander poured glasses of sherry and brought one to Sir Roger, who appeared less than pleased about the evening's entertainment. At present he stood staring morosely into the fire.

Taking the glass, Sir Roger thanked his lordship, then sighed. "You know you didn't have to accept Westoke's invitation simply because you told Grandfather you would introduce me to all the females in the neighborhood. The earl's type, more often than not, has given me the cut direct in Town."

Alexander shook his head, then took a sip of his sherry. "Frankly, I was curious about my neighbors. I have yet to meet any of them." In truth, a certain Mr. Akers had sparked his curiosity more than any other.

"But you needn't worry. I won't force you to stand up with any of the young ladies."

Sir Roger made a mock face at his friend and then stared into the tiny glass of amber liquid. "Did you know there was something of an understanding between Westoke and Miss Addington? Neville told me about it on the way back from the tailor's this afternoon."

Suddenly Alex understood his friend's reluctance to attend the party. He'd become enamored with a woman promised elsewhere. Knowing his aunt's distaste for Roger, Alex was tempted to let the impression stand, yet he didn't wish his friend made unhappy over a misunderstanding.

"I would say that is something of an overstatement. I think the fathers once wished for a match, and I think Lady Landry has set her heart on her daughter being a countess, but the earl seemed uninterested in my cousin this afternoon. When I offered to send for her, he declined, saying he couldn't stay. Not exactly the actions of an ardent lover or even one duty bound."

Just then Neville entered the room, interrupting the gentlemen's conversation. He spread his arms and turned around like a young girl about to go to her first ball. "I think even that fellow Brummell would be cast into the shade by my new coat."

Alexander laughed, knowing that the great arbiter of fashion would likely have a stroke to know his clothes had been compared to the work of a country tailor from Holt who had quickly sewn the blue evening coat at the baron's request and for a great deal of money. It had been only fair that if the young ladies were to receive new apparel, then so should Neville.

"You shall have all the young ladies swooning, my boy," Alex teased.

An optimistic look settled in the boy's blue eyes, and

both gentlemen knew the lad was hoping Lady Blythe would note the difference.

The ladies arrived at that moment, and all thoughts of the earl's sister and Neville flew from the baron's mind as he beheld Miss Rochelle. She was a vision in pink. He couldn't take his eyes from her, and he suddenly remembered the warm feel of her lips under his last night. As the circumstances of the kiss flooded his mind, his suspicion about the young lady and Akers returned.

Lady Margaret announced, "Shall we go meet what constitutes Society in Cley?"

The gentlemen ushered the ladies out to the two waiting coaches. Some thirty minutes later, as they stepped down from the carriages, Alex was surprised at the size of Lord Westoke's affair. Westwood Manor, a great Tudor home, had been built well inland from the marshes. Nearly every window in the house appeared to be glowing with light. The baron had been led to believe it was a small private party, but it appeared the earl had invited most of the neighborhood, if the number of carriages lined up along the drive were any indication.

They were ushered into a cavernous drawing room full of people. Within minutes the earl, his beautiful sister, and a rather plain young lady whose drab brown hair was scraped back from her face, arrived to welcome them.

Ignoring much of the Chase's party, Westoke said, "Lord Landry, allow me to present my sister, Lady Blythe Crane. My dear, Baron Landry."

Alexander could see the fear in the young beauty's blue eyes. In an intuitive flash, he knew she was afraid he would reveal they had encountered one another once before, and under circumstances little to her credit. But he would never do Neville such a turn. "Lady

Blythe, I am delighted to meet you and"—he looked deliberately at the lady who'd been ignored at her side—"your companion?"

Westoke, remembering himself, said, "This is our cousin, Miss Nora Crane."

"Delighted, Miss Crane. Pray allow me to present Lady Margaret, Dowager Countess of Wotherford, Sir Roger Howard, and of course you know my cousin and the Rochelles."

The earl's sister scarcely acknowledged anyone once she realized the baron would keep her secret. Instead, she slid her arm through his, then looked up at him coquettishly through her lashes. "Do allow me to introduce you to all our friends and neighbors, my lord."

Alexander had little choice but to be dragged about the room by the determined miss. He took note that Neville stood sullenly in conversation with Miss Crane, never taking his gaze from the raven-haired minx leading Alex about the room. There were a surprising number of people to be met. After introductions to an Admiral Kaplan, a difficult task since the man's hearing had failed due to cannon fire, Alex's gaze strayed in search of Valara, while the leathery old seaman began to bellow a tale of his adventures with Nelson in Egypt.

Valara stood in deep conversation with a gentleman with a vague but pleasant expression on his handsome face. He was nodding his head in agreement with whatever the young lady was telling him. Surely this wasn't Akers, for the man was forty if he was a day.

Curious, he asked Lady Blythe, "Who is the gentleman speaking with Miss Rochelle?"

A frown marred her lovely face to find him interested in another female. Then she searched the room. "Oh, him. Merely Mr. Ronald Akers. I am surprised he came, for he rarely attends the social happenings in Cley. You needn't pay much heed to the man. He owns a small estate on the far side of yours. As I remember, he is mad for birds." Lady Blythe grimaced. "When we were children, we went to his dovecote once, and the smell was simply awful. I was ill for the rest of the day. I believe he is trying to breed the fastest bird in England or some such foolish notion." She lowered her voice and continued, "He's rather odd, but my brother's secretary invited everyone to meet you."

After that, Alexander had little time to observe the gentleman. The butler announced dinner, and Alex ushered Lady Blythe into the cavernous dining room. To his dismay, he found himself seated to the young lady's left. Lady Margaret sat next to Westoke at the opposite end of the table. While the footmen served turtle soup, Alex's gaze roved over the guests, and he discovered Miss Rochelle beside her brother at the center of the table. It spoke volumes about their status in Cley society. Alexander found strange comfort in the fact Mr. Akers was seated some three guests away from Valara.

The meal seemed to drag as Lady Blythe flirted with the baron and gossiped with the rotund squire to her right, all the while eating copious amounts of each course. He marveled at her slender frame; only her jaw seemed to get a great deal of exercise.

Relief flooded Alexander when the earl suggested the ladies retire and the cloth be removed. He'd heard far too much about Bath, the price of French silk, and the peccadilloes of people he didn't know. After the ladies departed, he took his brandy and moved around the table to join Sir Roger. The gentlemen mingled and mixed, and soon Alexander was introduced to his nearest neighbor, Mr. Akers. He was handsome in a boyish way, despite the radiating lines denoting his age. He possessed sandy brown curls about a tanned face and large gray eyes that were thickly lashed.

"My lord." His neighbor bowed. "I hope you will

forgive me for not calling to welcome you to the neighborhood, but spring is my busiest time, what with all the new hatchlings." The gentleman then proceeded to discourse on the breeding, the care, and the feeding of pigeons for some ten minutes. Alexander could only wonder that this man snared Miss Rochelle's affections. Or was it some other gentleman she'd gone to meet that night at the mill?

"You must come with Miss Rochelle the next time she visits, for she is a bird fancier as well."

Suddenly Alex didn't want to know anymore about birds or Miss Rochelle's visits. It only confirmed his worst suspicions that the lady was involved with the gentleman. He quickly changed the subject."I understand you are something of a sailor, Mr. Akers."

Akers's face brightened. "That I am. I've a neat little sloop harbored at Cley. You and your friend must come sailing with me sometime and bring Mr. Rochelle. The boy seems to have a natural bent for the sea."

The baron politely accepted the invitation, but suspected it would be some time before he would be free to engage in such pleasurable activities. Or was he afraid Miss Rochelle might wish to join them to be with her particular friend?

The earl announced the ladies were waiting to dance, and the gentlemen made their way to the ballroom. A string quartet could be heard warming up. As they entered the ballroom, the red watered silk walls suddenly gave Alexander the impression he had stepped into the realm of the underworld of the Roman gods he'd read about as a lad.

Spying Lady Margaret in conversation with Miss Rochelle, he and Sir Roger made their way to the ladies. At that moment, young Neville brushed by them, cutting a straight path for Lady Blythe, who stood in conversation with the fashionable young wife of a viscount.

Miss Crane remained mutely at her side, looking a bit like a crow lost among a flock of peacocks.

The boy came to a halt directly in front of his old childhood companion and executed an awkward bow. "Would you do me the honor of dancing the first set with me, Lady Blythe?"

A shadow of annoyance passed over her face before she hissed, "Oh, for heaven's sake, Nev, do stop being such a besotted ninny. I must save my dances for eligible gentlemen, and you certainly are not one of those." She pushed Miss Crane forward. "Here, dance with Nora. She is not likely to be asked in her station."

Alexander watched the earl's sister heedlessly trample on Neville's heart, surprised the chit could be so cruel to such an old friend. But Mr. Rochelle proved to be more game than one might have thought for his tender years. Though his face flushed bright red, he squared his shoulders and managed to offer his arm to the equally mortified companion with dignity. "I should be delighted, Miss Crane."

As the pair left to join the others forming lines for the dance, Lady Margaret remarked, "What a spiteful little cat. Someone needs to teach that miss a lesson."

Valara Rochelle's cheeks were as bright as her brother's. "It seems Bly left her heart behind with her childhood."

Alexander heartily agreed. Then he realized Lady Blythe's gaze was locked on him. She lingered a moment dimpling at him, a come-hither look in her eyes. When he didn't react, she hurried forward. Before he had the least time to act, she was before him, fluttering her lashes. "Do not tell me you don't intend to dance, Lord Landry. You will disappoint all the ladies if that is the case."

After what he'd just witnessed, Alex was determined not to take the dance floor with the callous little jade.

"I do intend to dance. I came to remind Miss Rochelle she promised to save the first dance for me."

He held out his hand as the lady's startled gaze flew to his face. She quickly recovered herself and placed her hand atop his. "So I did. You will excuse us, Lady Margaret."

Alexander heard the dowager chuckle as he led Miss Rochelle to the line. From the corner of his eye, he saw Lady Blythe storm off to inveigle a young man in a claret evening coat to dance with her. Looking back to Valara, who stood opposite him, he noted her gaze was on her brother further down the line.

"He will survive, you know. First love is always the most painful."

Her blue gaze returned to his face and their eyes locked. It was as if some unspoken emotion seemed to dance on the air between them. He seemed on the verge of learning some profound truth about her. Then, to his disappointment, she lowered her lashes and said softly, "I suppose that is true."

The small orchestra began to play, and the dancers performed credibly despite the myriad emotions running through the company. Alexander hoped he would be able to find time alone with Valara to understand her enigmatic look when he'd spoken of first love.

When the dance ended, Alexander escorted the young lady back to Lady Margaret, who, with the elderly women, had settled into the gilt chairs that lined the walls.

Valara sat beside her, then began to search the room for her brother. "Do you see Neville?"

"Why, he left the room when the music had scarcely ended." Lady Margaret fanned herself, showing little concern for the young man. Like most ladies her age, she well knew navigating the intricacies of romance was difficult for all concerned, but most people managed to make it into the safe harbor of marriage. Therefore one needn't worry unduly.

Valara rose and made as if to follow, but Alexander reached out and detained her. "Perhaps he needs a few moments to gather himself."

She worried her lip a moment with her teeth, then shook her head. "He is so young and vulnerable. I don't think he should be alone."

Lady Margaret patted the seat beside her. "He's not a child, my dear. You cannot protect him from life's little bumps and bruises. Besides, that companion of Lady Blythe's followed him. She will certainly come and tell you if he needs one of us. For my part, I think he has proven himself made of sterner stuff than one would expect at his age. Look on the bright side. He now sees Lady Blythe for the heartless little wench she is."

Alexander watched Valara sink back onto the edge of the gilt chair, but he could see she was still torn. He leaned down and whispered, "If he does not return soon, we shall go and find him."

Her face flushed pink with gratitude. "Thank you."

Alexander straightened suddenly when he was overwhelmed with the desire to kiss her upturned face. What was the matter with him? There were too many secrets in Valara Rochelle's life for him to be tumbling head over heels in love with her.

He turned to watch the door, trying to concentrate on the matter at hand—Neville and his broken heart. Likely the boy would return soon and wish to depart. He fully understood Valara's worry for her sibling. When Adriana and Amy had hurt as children, he'd wanted to do all in his power to ease that pain. Unfortunately, Miss Rochelle would have to accept that only time would ease Neville's dashed hopes.

Nine

Miss Nora Crane peered into the darkness, searching for Mr. Rochelle, but the glow of the lanterns at the front doors revealed nothing but the empty expanse of the front drive, well-manicured lawns, and rows of empty carriages. He'd managed to disappear in a matter of minutes, yet he'd come this way.

Whatever was she doing out here? She hardly knew the young man, but her cousin's cruel words kept ringing in her ears. Nora knew she must find him and do what she could to ease his pain and humiliation—to let him know Lady Blythe Crane was not worth so much as a single tear. Not that young men would admit to such.

This had seemed the longest week of Nora's life. She hadn't wanted to come to Westwood to be a companion to her spoiled cousin, but plain spinsterish daughters of younger sons had little choice in such matters. Her father had insisted, reminding her he was depending on Westoke to help send her brothers to Oxford. From the beginning, she'd known she could do little to rein in Blythe. But, Nora decided, the least she could do was to help the innocent victims left in her cousin's wake.

Nora turned to one of the blue-and-gold liveried footmen on duty. "Did a young man pass this way?"

"Aye, miss, 'twas Mr. Rochelle from the Chase." The servant pointed to the west. "Headed that direction, he did. Might be trying to walk home, from the looks of him."

With all her thoughts centered on the nice boy who had danced with her, she lifted her gown and set out across the lawn in the direction the footman had indicated. She didn't truly think he would walk all the way back to Landry Chase. If her memory held, she thought there was a small summerhouse and a pond in this direction. More likely he had gone there to lick his wounds.

She walked briskly despite the darkness, since she was a country girl and not the least bit afraid of venturing away from the manor. As she rounded a large sculpted shrub, she thought she caught a flash of his white cravat ahead, which made her hurry on. She entered a grove of birch trees. Having forged deep into the woods, she stopped, suddenly realizing how very dark it truly was. Looking over her shoulder, she could no longer see the lights from Westwood Manor through the dense shrubbery and trees.

The cracking of a branch made her spin round, yet she could see nothing. "Mr. Rochelle, is that you?" she called softly. There was no reply.

Her heart began pounding, for she was quite lost in the night. Ahead she could barely make out an open meadow, and suddenly she didn't want to be in the overwhelming darkness of the grove. Perhaps if she went forward she could find the road and return to Westwood.

Within minutes she stepped into the open air of a field, where the clear starlit skies no longer seemed to drain her courage. She discerned a fence ahead, and relief flooded through her. As much as she wanted to help Mr. Rochelle, she knew she must go back to Blythe and the manor. The earl would be furious if he knew she'd been so foolish as to go after a lovesick boy.

On reaching the fence, she discovered it was too high to climb, reaching well above her head, so she searched for a gate. She hoped she was near the front of the estate, but it had been years since she'd last visited Westwood, and she found herself completely disoriented. All she could be certain of was that if she followed the fence line, she would find a way back home.

At last she came to an arched portal with a rusted iron gate. Relieved, she lifted the latch and stepped through. When she turned to reset the latch, the nicker of a horse sounded behind her. She whirled in fright.

In the darkness, she saw the vague silhouettes of several people and animals before a flash of pain exploded in her head as something struck her. Her knees gave way and she crumpled to the ground as a voice called, "What have you done, you fool?"

Miss Nora Crane sank into oblivion.

By the end of the second set, Valara would no longer be delayed. "I am going to find my brother."

"Very well." His lordship stepped to her side from the nearby wall, where he'd remained during the new round of dancing. "I shall accompany you."

She thanked him, then followed him across the room. In some ways his kindness to her and her brother made it harder for her to bear her situation. His comments about first love were true. She'd realized standing there on the dance floor that she was in love with a man whom circumstances dictated he marry someone else. She was going to be hurt, but she could do nothing to change who they were, a poor relation and a half-pay officer who'd inherited a mountain of debt.

Putting such dark realities from her mind, she turned

her thoughts to finding her brother. As they made their way to the ballroom door, she noted Sir Roger standing with his arms crossed over his chest, clearly not enjoying the entertainment. Seeing them approach, he straightened. "Are we leaving?" His tone was hopeful.

The baron explained they were looking for young Rochelle, who'd been gone from the ballroom for some twenty minutes. Sir Roger offered to join in the search. It took another ten minutes of looking in the manor's public rooms before they questioned the footman on the portico, who informed them both Mr. Rochelle and Miss Crane had left via the front door, albeit separately, heading west.

"Where the devil could that young cawker be going?" Sir Roger moved down the front steps, peering into the darkness.

"Possibly back home," Valara suggested. "There is a path we used as children to move back and forth between the two estates. One can walk to the Chase from here in under thirty minutes."

"Would he leave without telling anyone? I have tried to convince you all it's not safe on the marshes at night." Disapproval was evident in Lord Landry's voice, but Valara couldn't bring herself to look at him, knowing he was subtly reminding her of their last meeting in the dark.

"Neville was upset. I cannot know for certain what was in his mind. Surely nothing would happen to him in so short a distance." But in her heart Valara knew that during the dark of the moon anything could happen on the marshes, and she was afraid.

Landry turned to Sir Roger. "I don't like the idea of him out there alone. Between Waite and the local Gentlemen he might tumble into trouble or be hurt. Give my regrets to Lord Westoke and tell him I was called away. See the ladies home safely when they are ready."

Sir Roger hurried back up the stairs into the manor at once, eager to do as he was bid. It was clear that the sooner he was gone from under the earl's roof, the happier he would be.

"I am going with you." Valara laid a restraining hand on his lordship's sleeve as he was about to leave. A surprising shock seemed to run up her arm, and she drew back instantly even as she refused to be left behind.

There was only a moment's pause as his dark gaze raked her. "Very well." He turned to the footman. "We need a small lantern."

The servant disappeared. Alexander took note of the questioning look on Valara's face. "I don't want to give Captain Waite any reason to accuse us of any nefarious doings while we search for Neville."

She nodded her head, then turned and stared into the darkness and prayed that wherever Nev had gone, he had gotten there safely.

Within minutes, the footman returned with a small lantern. His lordship thanked the man then, turned and handed Valara the small brass light. "Show me this path to the Chase."

They set out at once, his lordship keeping pace with her as she moved rapidly westward. It had been years since she'd roved over the grounds of Westwood, but the path was still clearly visible in the lantern light, making her wonder who had been tramping the byways, since Lady Blythe and the earl were rarely in residence. The servants, no doubt. She led the baron through the woods and fields to a small arched gateway in the stone wall.

She held the lantern high and indicated the portal. "This gate opens to the main roadway. On the other side there is a break in the Chase's fence. The stones tumbled years ago and were never repaired."

Landry stepped to the gate and lifted the latch, but

when he tried to push it open, it resisted. "Bring the lantern closer."

Valara held the light up to the decorative iron gate and peered through. She gasped, "It's Miss Crane on the ground, and she's hurt."

His lordship pulled the gate in the opposite direction. It protested loudly, but at last it opened wide enough for them to slip through. They knelt beside Lady Blythe's companion. "She's been attacked and is bleeding. The Gentlemen's work, no doubt," Lord Landry announced as he lifted his hand from her head and came away with blood on his fingertips.

"I need a makeshift bandage to stem the bleeding." Valara leaned close and could see the wound was at the edge of the woman's hairline.

Without hesitation, Alexander untied his cravat and passed it to Valara. She gave him the lantern and quickly bound the young lady's head. "We must have the doctor look at this at once."

"I shall carry her, but which manor house are we closest to at this moment?" He handed the lantern back to Valara, then leaned over and scooped the unconscious woman into his arms.

In the light, she caught the twinkle of a gold medallion at his open collar, and wondered about its significance momentarily before her thoughts returned to the matter at hand. "We must continue on the path for home. Neville might be hurt somewhere along the way." There was a desperate urgency in her voice.

"Lead the way."

They crossed the road and stepped onto his lordship's lands. After a ten-minute walk, they arrived in the Great Hall, to the startled surprise of Bainbridge and the other footmen. Lord Landry ordered the doctor be summoned for Miss Crane at once and word be sent to the earl that his cousin was at the Chase and injured.

As the footman hurried away, Valara inquired about her brother.

"Mr. Neville, miss? Why, he left with you to go to Westwood. We've not seen him since." Bainbridge looked baffled.

Valara's heart plummeted. Where had her brother disappeared to?

Sir Roger entered the ballroom, halting at the edge of the dance floor to search for the ladies of the Chase. He spied Elaina at once, doing a country dance with a young man in regimentals. Jealousy filled his chest. He wanted to be the one holding her hand, leading her through the intricate steps.

Then he reminded himself she was intended for Lord Westoke. There was no point in beating his head against a brick wall. She might flirt with the grandson of a Cit, but she would do what was best by marrying into an old, distinguished family. He'd been through it all before in London. His grandfather was deluding himself if he thought Roger might find a genteel bride who would overlook his humble antecedents.

He dragged his gaze from Elaina and searched for Lady Margaret. Spotting the dowager in conversation with another woman, he strode across the room and bowed. Then, in a low voice, he quickly relayed Alexander's message.

"Called away?" The lady knit her bows a moment, then asked, "Does this have something to do with Neville's wounded pride?"

Sir Roger leaned close. "They think he may have taken the path home between the two estates. Alex and Miss Rochelle have followed him to make certain he arrives home unharmed. I am to escort you ladies home."

"Then the boy is well taken care of and there is no

need to rush. Miss Addington must finish her dance. Besides, don't you wish to take the floor with her?" The dowager gave him a knowing smile.

The gentleman took a breath, his gaze veering to the wallpaper behind her ladyship as he shook his head. "No doubt she would much rather dance with the man who will be her future husband, madam. I rarely take the floor."

Her ladyship tilted her head and studied the young man through narrowed eyes. "I see." With a slight nod of her head, she crossed her hands and tapped her foot to the music while they awaited the end of the set. To the casual observer, she appeared to be watching the dancers move down the floor in time with the music but, in truth, the lady's mind was busy at her favorite occupation, matchmaking.

Some ten minutes later, the soldier escorted Miss Addington back to her chaperon. After he bowed and departed, the dowager announced, "I fear we must leave, my dear."

Elaina's gaze flew to Sir Roger. "But I have not danced . . ." Her voice trailed off on seeing the frozen look on the baronet's face. Straightening, she addressed Lady Margaret. "Is there some reason we must depart early?"

The countess quickly explained that Mr. Rochelle had disappeared and the others were searching for him on the path to the Chase.

"Then we must return home at once."

The three remaining members of the party from the Chase went to bid Lord Westoke farewell. He stood in conversation with several rowdy young bucks from the neighborhood, an empty champagne glass in his hand.

"Lord Landry *and* Miss Rochelle called away together? How very odd." His bloodshot eyes narrowed, but his tone implied a great deal when he continued, "But then perhaps not very strange after the rumors floating about tonight. Seems I wasted my blunt on this party." The earl offered no explanation of his remarks, nor did he offer to walk them to their vehicle. Instead he turned and fell back into conversation with his companions.

"Come, ladies," the baronet said, ushering them from the ballroom.

Lady Margaret was all agog. "What rumors can he mean?"

Elaina shook her head, caring little in the misery of her rebuff by Sir Roger. "There is little to do in Cley but gossip. Pay no heed to anything you hear."

Outside, to their surprise, Sir Roger closed the door to the carriage after they were settled. "I shall ride in the second coach." He strode off into the darkness.

Her ladyship clucked. "Young people! You do manage to have more misunderstandings than two warring nations. It quite tires me out. But don't fear, I shall see that all comes right in the end, if you don't sort it out."

Elaina scarcely took note of her ladyship's chatter. She couldn't quite understand what had happened to make Sir Roger so cold. Why hadn't he wanted to dance with her? The night had been quite ruined, and she was glad they were going home.

She sat up straight as she realized half of their party had failed to return home in the safety of their carriages. She suddenly hoped that Lara, Nev, and Alexander had made it back to Chase unharmed. There was certainly no guarantee on a moonless night on the marshes.

The case clock in the hall had just chimed the midnight hour when the sounds of a carriage echoed in the Great Hall of Landry Chase. Valara dashed to the drawing room door, then waited with bated breath.

When Bainbridge opened the door, she uttered a cry of relief as her brother stepped into the hall, handing the butler his hat and coat as casually as if he'd just returned from a morning walk. She dashed across the marble floor and threw herself into Neville's arms. "Where have you been?"

"At Westwood Manor. You took your leave while I was out at the pond." Neville's tone was incensed. "I had to beg a ride from Admiral Kaplan, who is deaf as a stump and nearly ruptured my ears with his incessant sea tales in his closed carriage. Where did everyone go?"

"Looking for you, silly. When you left the ballroom so suddenly, everyone thought you had decided to walk home." Valara drew back, taking in every feature of his beloved face, but not releasing him from her arms. Miss Crane's attack had unnerved Valara far more than she realized.

"Walked home! I didn't take complete leave of my wits or my manners, dear sister. I would have told you had I decided to leave. I just strolled down to the pond . . . well, to do some thinking . . . about things." The boy's flushed face filled with hurt pride.

Hearing approaching footsteps, Valara released him from the embrace and turned to see Lord Landry and the others. "He is safe and unharmed," she announced to everyone with relief.

Neville looked at the worried faces and his cheeks grew pink. "I—I'm dreadfully sorry if I gave you all a scare. Just needed some time alone."

Lord Landry nodded, his visage reflecting only concern, not anger. "I understand, but I think it should be Miss Crane to whom you apologize. She was worried about you, as well, and followed you. Only she lost her way in the dark and was attacked on the road between the two estates."

Neville's face drained of color.

His lordship added, "The doctor has been here, and she will be fine after a few days' rest." He looked about at the other faces. "I think we could all use some, after such a night."

There was a murmur of agreement. No one needed any urging to say their good nights and retire to their rooms. Exhausted by the night's nerve-racking events, Valara slipped into bed, promising herself to rise early. She had to go to the mill to put the money in the secret box for Monsieur Dubois. He would be back here to-morrow night, so there could be no further delay.

The following morning, Valara's clock was just chiming seven when she quietly slipped from her room. She was dressed in her black mourning gown and her sturdy half boots, the packet of money safely hidden in the pocket of her underskirt. She made her way to the front hall and was halfway down the stairs when Lord Landry stepped from the library.

His brows rose in surprise. "Good morning, Miss Rochelle. I didn't expect to see anyone this early."

Valara's heart plummeted. Neither had she. She took a deep breath and manufactured an excuse for her unexpected appearance at such an hour. "I was hoping to get an early start since we now have two invalids to care for. What has you out and about so early, sir?"

"I am meeting the steward and a master carpenter from Norwich at the mill this morning. The fellow will be taking measurements for the new main spar we need to put the mill back in operation. I hoped to ask him some questions about modernizing before he starts work, since I am certain he will be there much of the day going over the mill's wooden cogs to see if any need replacing." The gentleman smiled at her. "Won't you join me for breakfast?"

The news his lordship imparted only made Valara's day a little more bleak. If men would be working at the mill all day, she wouldn't be able to sneak away until tonight. It meant another dark trip across the fields to the edge of the marsh, risking dangerous encounters with smugglers or tidesmen or both.

Looking at the baron's handsome face, she realized there was little she could do about the matter this morning. She might as well have breakfast with him. "I believe I shall."

Valara enjoyed a pleasant half hour with Lord Landry, listening to all his plans for improving the estate. She even offered a few suggestions herself. Mr. Bailey arrived promptly at half past seven and took his lordship off to the mill.

Finishing her coffee alone, watching the sun rise above the trees through the breakfast parlor windows, she experienced a lovely vision of what life might be like if she were married to Alexander. Leisurely morning breakfasts, walks together in the gardens in the afternoon, entertaining neighbors and relatives, then—her cheeks flushed warmly when her thoughts roved to nights in those strong arms. She rose abruptly, almost causing her chair to overturn. She had no business torturing herself with such images. He would need a great deal of money to implement his plans, and that would require a wealthy wife.

She returned her coffee cup to the saucer with a loud clatter and hurried from the room. It was best to keep busy, not to worry about tonight's outcome. Most of all, not to think of his lordship.

She went to her room and returned the packet of money to her desk drawer, then went to Miss Crane's door and scratched lightly, not wishing to wake her if she were asleep. But that young lady called for her to enter immediately.

Valara peered round the door to discover Lord Westoke's cousin sitting up, looking a bit confused.

"Good morning, Miss Crane. How are you feeling to-day?"

"Miss Rochelle? H-how did I"—she looked about the large room done with pale yellow flowered paper and matching hangings. Before she could even finish the sentence, a dawning expression settled on her face. "Why, I am at Landry Chase. Did your brother make it here safely last night?"

"He did, but I fear you did not. Do you know who attacked you?" Valara came to straighten the bedcovers as the young lady's face puckered in thought. Miss Crane's brown hair lay loose about her shoulders, making her appear almost handsome, if not pretty.

She shook her head, then put her hand to the tender swelling at the edge of her scalp as she slumped back against the pillows. "I think it may have been smugglers, yet the one voice I heard was cultured." She sighed, then shrugged her shoulders and let her hand drop back to the covers. "I couldn't see any faces in the dark."

"Never mind, my dear. What you need is something to eat. I shall go to the kitchens and have them prepare some tea and toast to start."

The young lady smiled. "Tea would be most welcome."

Valara hurried downstairs and informed Cook of the simple requirements. Within a few minutes, a tray held the requested items, as well as a dish of strawberry jam and a small posy of wildflowers. Valara took the meal back to Miss Crane, then sat in a chair beside her as the recovering lady sipped her tea and picked at the toast, giving the pair a chance to become acquainted.

It soon became clear that life at Westwood Manor was no treat for Nora Crane. She didn't openly complain about her treatment, but Valara was able to read between the lines. As much as Lord Westoke might need a companion for Lady Blythe, the lady had other ideas.

It appeared she mostly ignored Nora. When forced to take note, she used her cousin like a menial, asking her to do tasks more suited to a maid. Valara decided that all two years of schooling had taught their old friend was to be a spoiled tyrant.

Miss Crane pushed her half-finished breakfast aside as a soft scratching sounded on the door. Valara went to answer it and discovered Elaina, looking quite glum.

"Whatever has you blue-deviled?"

"Nothing. I just didn't sleep well," Elaina snapped. She stepped into the room and, in a far from cheerful voice, inquired, "Good morning, Miss Crane. How are you feeling today?"

"I have a slight headache, but other than that I am well. Do either of you know if my cousin was informed of my accident?" Nora plucked nervously at the blanket. "I cannot be away from Westwood long, for there are my duties."

Valara joined her cousin, who'd moved to the foot of the Nora's bed. "A message was sent last night, but the footman said there was no answer. No doubt Lady Blythe will come today to bring your clothes, for I fear your gown was ruined by the brambles as Lord Landry carried you through the home wood. But you mustn't think of trying to rise too soon, for you were knocked unconscious."

Elaina smiled at Nora. "You needn't worry that the earl or his sister would expect you back before you are fully recovered."

The look on Nora's face told Valara that would be exactly what Lord Westoke and his spoiled sister would expect of a poor relation. "Don't worry. We shall ask the baron to convince your cousin you need until the end of the week to recover."

A sudden disturbance in the hall outside the bed-chamber caused everyone to stop and listen. The butler could be heard arguing with someone. At last a sharp knock sounded on the door. Elaina strode forward and opened it. "What is it, Bainbridge?"

From her position beside the bed, Valara could see little, but she heard Mr. Binion's angry voice. "I demand to see Miss Rochelle at once."

Then, to her surprise, she recognized Mr. Akers's voice. "I say, Binion, what is this all about? Ain't the thing to be barging upstairs in someone's home. The ladies may not be home to visitors, if you take my meaning."

Valara hurried to the door, surprised to find not one but two gentlemen in the upstairs hall.

On seeing her beside her cousin, Mr. Binion cried, "There you are. I must have a few words in private with you." His tone was sharp.

Bainbridge's hand was planted in the middle of the clergyman's chest. The butler's lined face was a picture of distress at having failed in his duty. "Miss Rochelle, I tried to have the reverend wait downstairs with Mr. Akers, but he wouldn't listen."

Valara closed the door to Miss Crane's room and shot an earnest glance at her cousin before she said, "Don't worry, Bainbridge. I shall speak with Mr. Binion."

Elaina, realizing what was required, stepped forward. "Mr. Akers, come. We shall go to the green drawing room and allow the vicar to have his say."

While her cousin led their neighbor down the hall, Valara eyed the clergyman curiously, then announced, "Bainbridge, I shall use the yellow salon. Pray take tea to my cousin and Mr. Akers. We shall join them later, if that is Mr. Binion's wish. Also, send a maid up to sit with Miss Crane."

The butler released his hold, but still glared at the grim-faced young vicar. "Very good, miss. This way, sir."

Once in the small formal salon off the front hall, she settled in a yellow damask chair and gestured for the clergyman to take the sofa. She couldn't imagine what had him in such a taking. He was clearly distressed, for his hands were crushing the brim of his round hat. "Has something dreadful happened at the orphanage, sir?"

Refusing the seat, he shook his head before tossing his hat on the sofa. He began to pace before her as he launched into speech. "When I heard the first rumor, I dismissed it as total nonsense, Miss Rochelle. I thought it all a hum or one of that fool Riding Officer's lies. The very idea of you engaged in a tryst on the marshes with his lordship was beyond the realm of possibility for the proper young woman I know."

He paused and stared at her as if she had suddenly grown horns. "But I have just come from a meeting with Westoke about the living in Cley. His lordship informs me you blatantly disappeared from his party last night alone with his lordship. Are you trying to completely ruin your reputation? Will you so willingly surrender everything a woman holds dear to a man who has done little with his life save gaming and adventuring?"

Valara's back stiffened. "Mr. Binion, I don't have to explain my actions to you. But if you must know, my brother disappeared last night and Lord Landry went to help me find him."

"Disappeared! Ha!" the clergy scoffed, his thin face grown pink. "It was Neville looking for you at the end of the ball, as I hear the matter. I cannot believe you would be so foolish as to allow this underbred baron to take advantage of your goodness. What am I to think?"

Angry now to be taken to task by someone who was a mere acquaintance and for something she hadn't done, Valara rose and marched to the door, yanking it open. "Mr. Binion, I care not what you think of me, but how dare you slander his lordship with idle gossip? Lord Landry has been excessively kind to everyone since he arrived here, especially to my brother and me, to whom he owes no responsibility whatsoever. I won't stand here and allow you to impugn him or me falsely. Leave at once."

All the color drained from Binion's face. He moved to stand in front of her. "Miss Rochelle, if you will only give me reasonable explanations for these tales, I promise I shall forgive you for such youthful indiscretions."

"Forgive me!" Valara snapped. "Sir, I have done nothing that needs to be forgiven, and especially not by you." She marched to the sofa, grabbed his hat, and shoved it into his hands.

His face twisted in anger. "Don't be a fool. Beautiful you may be, but everyone knows Landry's pockets will need to be replenished by an heiress. It is only a matter of time before he takes stock and knows what he must do for the good of the estate. Don't think I shall want you once he has tossed you aside."

Valara was so angry she could barely speak. "Mr. Binion, it is my fondest wish that you never think of me again. Please leave."

The clergyman angrily grabbed her arms and shook her. "You must listen to me—"

"Is there a problem, Miss Rochelle?" Sir Roger stood at the foot of the stairs, glaring at the gaunt man who was besieging the young lady.

On seeing the gentleman, Binion released his hold.

"The vicar was just leaving, Sir Roger." Valara stepped away from the man she thought she'd known for so many years, but who'd become a violent stranger in an instant. She spied the butler exiting the green drawing room. "Bainbridge, show Mr. Binion to the door. He won't be joining us for tea . . . now or ever again."

There was almost a glow of satisfaction on the old servant's face as he ushered the glowering young man to the door.

"Thank you, Sir Roger. I fear Mr. Binion quite forgot

himself." She smoothed the skirts of her gown, giving her a moment to collect her thoughts. "Would you care to join Mr. Akers and Elaina in the green drawing room?"

A shuttered look settled on the baronet's face. "I think not, Miss Rochelle. You will excuse me, but I believe I prefer to go to the breakfast parlor and break my fast instead." The gentleman strode off down the hall without a backward glance.

Valara's mind was in too much of a whirl after her encounter with Mr. Binion to pay much heed to Sir Roger's fits and starts that morning. She debated as to whether she should go back to Miss Crane or join her cousin in the drawing room. Realizing Elaina had helped her out upstairs, Valara knew she mustn't leave her to entertain their guest alone. She moved to the door that led to where her cousin and Mr. Akers waited.

For a brief moment, she knew a strong urge to weep—not for the loss of Mr. Binion's good opinion, but for the truth of his words about Lord Landry. It took several moments, but at last she gathered herself sufficiently to join the others. Mr. Akers politely rose as she entered.

"I hope there is no crisis at Seaforth, Miss Rochelle."

All she could do was shake her head, still too angry with the clergyman to speak on the matter. She took a seat and gladly accepted the cup of tea her cousin offered her. Conversation became general, and at the end of fifteen minutes the gentleman rose.

"I won't overstay, for I have matters to handle at home, but I did wish to invite you all sailing on the morrow. If that is inconvenient or should it rain, tell his lordship I am at his disposal any time he might be free from his duties. I should very much like to show you the *White Gull*. I moved the sloop to Akers's Quay this morning, so if anyone is interested, be there by twelve."

Elaina and Valara thanked him, saying they would gladly inform Lord Landry and send word if the arrangements were acceptable. They escorted him to the door, which had barely closed after the gentleman's departure when one of the new maids arrived and bobbed a curtsy. "Pardon me, Miss Addington, but Miss Crane is askin' for you or Miss Rochelle."

The cousins exchanged a look, each worried their guest's health might have taken a turn for the worse. They hurried up to the lady's room, where they were bade to enter after they knocked.

Nora Crane sat up in bed the instant they entered. "I must speak with Lord Landry at once."

The two came to stand beside her bed. Valara asked, "Are you unwell?"

The lady in bed shook her head. Instead she gave a satisfied smile. "I know who the man was with the smugglers last night. I heard him in the hall earlier."

Valara's mind reeled. There had been three men in the hallway earlier—Bainbridge, Mr. Binion, and Mr. Akers. Who could Nora mean?

Ten

Lord Landry arrived back from the mill just before ten. He'd been much impressed with Mr. Hawkin's expertise and agreed with the changes the carpenter recommended for the mill. The man had declared that the building could be repaired and back in operation within the month. It was a positive step in having Landry Chase become profitable again. For the first time, Alex felt he'd truly accomplished something good for the estate.

Handing his hat and crop to Bainbridge, Alexander halted on his way to the library as his cousin, Elaina, appeared at the head of the stairs, gesturing at him to come. He strode up the stairs with little enthusiasm, fearful that only bad news could await, since she rarely sought him out.

"Landry, we saw you arrive from the upstairs windows. You must come to Miss Crane's room at once." Elaina's manner was urgent. She grasped the baron's arm and began to draw him down the hall.

"Has she taken ill?" Uneasiness settled in his lordship's stomach. The doctor had sworn there was no great injury to the girl.

"She is well enough, but wishes to speak with you at once."

They entered Miss Crane's room to find the young

lady propped up by numerous pillows, Miss Rochelle at her side. The injured lady modestly tugged her blankets higher as he moved to greet her.

"Lord Landry, I know who attacked me last night." There was an excited glitter in her brown eyes, but no doubt in her tone.

His lordship looked from his cousin to Miss Rochelle, but they, too, seemed to be waiting with bated breath to hear what Miss Crane was about to say. "You recognized someone in the dark?" he asked skeptically.

Nora shook her head. "No, but I distinctly heard a voice last night before I fell unconscious. This morning I heard the same man's voice in the hall."

Alexander frowned. Was it going to be one of the servants after all? "Who is the smuggler?"

"He was demanding to see Miss Rochelle, and I believe I heard the other gentleman call him Binion."

"Binion!" All three of the lady's visitors voiced the name at once.

Valara shook her head as she looked across at Alexander, her face full of doubt. "That cannot be. He is a clergyman."

Alexander moved to the window and gazed out. Men were well capable of doing things people might little expect. He'd seen savage things during the war from men who were quiet and reserved in ordinary life. It was possible Binion was that type. Alex turned to face the ladies. "Perhaps a wolf in sheep's clothing? How well does anyone know another?"

Across the room, Valara cheeks grew warm under his lordship's marked stare. The memory of her secret trip to the mill and the secrets she kept lay between them. He was right. Anyone could lead a different life away from the eyes of their neighbors.

Elaina gave a mirthless laugh. "That explains why he has been keeping the older boys long after they are employable. He is running a smuggling operation, and they are his helpers."

Valara put a hand to her head. The morning had been too full of shocks for her to cope with this new revelation. "I cannot believe he would risk the orphanage that is so important to him to involve himself and the boys in such a dangerous occupation. He is devoted to those boys."

Suddenly Landry turned from the window and strode across the room. At the door he paused, looking back over his shoulder. "I intend to find out the truth and put a stop to this smuggling business once and for all. I will not knowingly have my lands used or allow a bunch of innocent lads to risk their future for someone's personal gain."

As the gentleman exited the room, Valara dashed to the door and followed him into the hall. "Lord Landry."

Alexander halted, frowning as his gaze searched her face for some clue to her emotions. Was she worried about the vicar, who'd claimed to have an understanding with her? She was such an enigma he didn't know where her hopes lay, with the clergyman or the mysterious stranger she'd been meeting on the marsh. "What is it?"

"Please be careful. I have reason to know Mr. Binion can have a vile temper."

A smile touched his mouth and his gaze caressed her. "Why, *cara*, I would almost think you were worried about me."

The young lady's cheeks turned pink and she grew a bit flustered. "I-I am. Y-you have done much to help us all since you came."

A bit disappointed in her response, the baron reminded himself that at least she felt something for him. "Binion has too much to lose to risk violence, *cara*. I shall take Sir Roger with me. All will be well."

Alexander hurried down the stairs into the Great

Hall, only to find Sir Roger and young Neville in the green drawing room, conversing about the events of the previous night. Alex summoned Bainbridge, ordering fresh horses brought round.

Sir Roger rose, an eager expression on his face. "Going to see the vicar about his little dustup with Miss Rochelle this morning? I should like to join you."

The baron's eyes narrowed. "What exactly happened during his visit?" Miss Crane had mentioned Binion had been there but not why.

"The lady wouldn't say, but they were both very angry at the end of the meeting. She ordered him to leave and never return. He had her by the arms, trying to force her to listen, when I arrived."

Neville's face flushed pink, and he started to his feet. "He did what? How dare he put his hands on my sister?"

A menacing smile appeared on Alex's face. "I see I have one more thing to take the man to task for." He then quickly repeated what Miss Crane had just related upstairs.

Neville gasped. "By Jove, Waite had it right when he accused old Binny all those months ago. And here I thought the Riding Officer a complete fool, as did most of the townspeople. What do you intend to do?"

The baron drew on his riding gloves. "Pay the man a visit and make certain this dangerous business is stopped."

The boy put a restraining hand on Alexander's arm. "But what about the orphanage? I'm certain he did it to keep the orphanage open. I can assure you he doesn't have an avaricious bone in his pious body. I never thought I'd be saying this, but old Binny's the best thing that ever happened to homeless boys in Norfolk County. If you turn him in, what will happen to Seaforth?"

Alexander and Sir Roger exchanged a knowing look. Then the baron clapped a hand on Neville's shoulder.

"Don't worry. I shall make certain Seaforth has a bene-factor. One way or the other, the orphanage shall remain open."

"Can I come with you?" Neville asked hopefully.

"If you wish."

The gentlemen waited in silence while mounts were brought round, then rode to Seaforth forthwith. The old manor house looked quiet and peaceful as they approached, revealing none of its secrets to the casual observer.

After leaving their horses with a lad who was raking the gravel walk, Landry and the others entered the main hall. Alex gestured to Neville. "Which of these rooms is the library?"

The boy led the way and knocked. There was no summons, only shuffling sounds. Then a voice bade them enter. Alexander strode first into the room and was immediately struck by the group gathered and their guilty countenances.

Mr. Binion stood behind a desk, flanked by three young men long past the age of needing an orphanage. The baron recognized young Danny, looking frightened despite his great size.

"Planning your tactics for tonight, vicar?" Alex strode across the room, noting what looked like a map rolled up on the desk.

A scowl settled on the clergyman's face. "What are *you* doing here?"

"I've come to put a stop to your little nocturnal operation," the baron said, as Neville and Sir Roger moved to either side of him. "And to make certain you understand you are never to go near Miss Rochelle again."

Binion's face grew pale as he locked gazes with Lord Landry. The baron's eyes held a steely determination only a fool would ignore. Still, the vicar remained defiant. "I don't know what you mean about a night operation. As to Miss Rochelle, don't think I shall stand by and allow you to ruin her good name without giving her a warning."

A chill coiled deep in Alexander's gut with those words. Had his attempts to save Valara on the marsh endangered her reputation? Putting that aside for the moment, he said, "Don't play the fool, man. Miss Crane heard you speaking the night you struck her down."

Danny blurted out, "It weren't him, sir. It were me. Me and the other lads." He gestured to the two young men standing quietly beside him. "The reverend had nothing to do with any of it. 'Twas me what went to Yarmouth and met with me da's old mates. Ye can't be thinkin' of closin' the orphanage."

"Shut up, you young fool," Binion ordered. Then, realizing the boy had spilled all, the vicar sank into a chair, all the fight seeming to drain out of him. "I knew one day we might be caught, but there was no other way. The funds from the local parishes had all but dried up and most of the titled families didn't seem to care if my boys lived or died. The other families' pockets were too empty to give aid. I had to find the money somewhere, or we would have had to send some of the boys away." He rose, glaring at Alexander. "Do what you will to me, but leave these boys out of it. They were only doing what I ordered."

"You struck Miss Crane?" Alex glared at the clergyman.

Danny spoke before Binion could even open his mouth. "It were my doin', my lord. Mr. Binion was furious at me. I regretted doin' it and tried to make it naught but a tap. Is the young lady seriously hurt?"

"She is recovering nicely at the Chase. It was she who informed me who was involved." Alex grew quiet at all he'd learned. While he would never like the vicar, especially after the way he'd bullied Valara, there could be little doubt that the man's intentions for funding the orphanage had been honorable, if unlawful. No good would come from turning him in to Waite and, in fact, the orphanage might well be closed. Alex came to a quick decision.

"Binion, it is not my wish to betray you to the Riding Officer. I simply want to put an end to local smuggling. Someone is likely to be killed if you continue in this manner." The baron leaned forward, putting his hands on the desk to make his point. "My friends and I will say nothing about what we know. But you *must* cease your dealings with the Gentlemen this very day. In return, I shall become the benefactor of Seaforth."

"You?" Doubt filled the vicar's face, but he seemed to see something in Landry's eyes that told him the man was honest. "How is that possible?"

Alexander straightened. "Despite rumors to the contrary, I am a wealthy man, thanks to some wise investments of my funds by friends." He glanced briefly at Sir Roger. "It is a matter I would not wish bandied about the neighborhood."

"But why? It would only raise your worth in the eyes of Society." Binion's brow wrinkled. All knew a wealthy man could have his way in Society.

"I would rather be judged by my character than by my pockets, sir. My philanthropy to the orphanage I wish to be kept secret." His tone brooked no argument.

The vicar looked at the boys, who stood listening intently, then back to the baron, his face a study in conflict. "If you wish to be anonymous, it shall be so, but . . . there is a problem with what you demand. We have one last run to fulfill tonight, and it would be dangerous if we were to fail to meet the shipment. Dubois and his men are ruthless. They know where the orphanage is and have threatened the younger boys before."

Alexander pondered the dilemma. They could go to

Waite and inform him about the exact locale of the incoming shipment, but if the Frenchman or his men escaped capture, Binion would likely be targeted for death—or, worse, one of the lads working with him might be killed. Alex sighed, seeing no other way but to allow the final rendezvous. "You are certain you can convince this smuggler to let you out after tonight?"

The vicar nodded. "He's been afraid of my using the lads from the beginning. Thinks they are likely to be too free with information to the wrong people. Besides, that gives him a month to make other arrangements before the next waning of the moon."

Alexander looked at Roger, who nodded. "Then we will do our best to see that the Riding Officer is distracted while you convince the Frenchman you are finished after you deliver this final cargo."

"May God protect us." Mr. Binion stood up and hesitantly offered his lordship his hand. The unusual group of conspirators gathered round the desk as the vicar unrolled the map and discussed the coming night's operation.

It came as a surprise to no one that the mill was the meeting point. Alex shook his head. "I would think that is exactly where Waite will expect the landing to be."

Binion pointed at the map. "We rarely land there because it is so obvious. I've had the lads whisper in town that the dower cottage is the place best to avoid tonight. Besides, Dubois was adamant they would be landing at the mill or at Akers's Quay, which the farmer built scarcely half mile down the beach from the mill."

"Then we know where we don't want the dragoons." Alexander turned to his two companions. "Neville, I shall need you on the roof tonight, if you are willing." The baron wanted Valara's brother out of harm's way.

The boy's eyes glittered with excitement at being included. "Whatever you need, I shall do."

Smiling at his friend, Alexander arched one brow. "Are you game to play decoy?"

Sir Roger grinned. "I have always wanted a taste of adventure, and tonight I shall likely be fired upon. Who could resist?"

"Fired upon! Not if we are careful." Alexander hoped his warning to Captain Waite the night he'd captured Valara would make the man more circumspect about firing before he knew his target.

With the plan in place, the gentlemen departed the orphanage. As they rode back to the Chase, Alexander knew he was a fool to be involving himself in this business, but still there was that little race of excitement in his blood at the prospect of danger. He couldn't deny he missed the rough and tumble life of soldiering. Then he realized life at Landry Chase had been anything but dull.

His thoughts veered to Valara and the vicar's words. Had Alex's attempt to save her from the law only backfired and left her reputation in tatters? Should he do the honorable thing and offer for her? His pulse raced at the idea of making her his. He wanted her, had wanted her since that day in the ballroom when he'd helped her to her feet, yet her mysterious visit to the mill had left him wondering if she had given her heart elsewhere. He wanted no reluctant bride.

At that moment, the gates of Landry Chase came into view and Alex realized he could settle all his worries about Valara after tonight's escapade. He said, "Gentlemen, I would prefer the ladies know nothing of our little adventure this evening."

All the gentlemen nodded in agreement.

Valara stood at the window, watching and waiting for the return of the gentlemen. Her mind still couldn't quite grasp the idea that Mr. Binion was involved in smuggling. Yet she knew the man well enough to know why he would do such a thing—Seaforth Orphanage. Would Lord Landry realize that as well and do nothing rash?

When her thoughts turned to his lordship, she couldn't help but savor the way he'd called her *cara* in the upstairs hall before he'd departed. The word had felt almost like a caress. Was she deluding herself that he held her in some affection?

A knock at the door interrupted Valara's musings. Lady Margaret entered, fashionably dressed in a simple green morning gown trimmed with Belgian lace. "There you are, my dear." She paused and eyed the young lady's black gown with critical eyes. "I must put some of Alexander's maids to helping Lisette and her assistant, for that gown is utterly dreadful. Oh, but never mind about that for now. I have been searching for you. Where is your cousin?"

"Aunt Belinda called Ellie to her room to make an accounting about Lord Westoke's party. I fear she won't be happy with the story my cousin has to tell. No doubt my aunt will summon Neville to rake him over the coals for having inadvertently caused us to leave early."

Her ladyship nodded, then changed the subject. "What are we to do about your cousin and Sir Roger?"

"I beg your pardon?" Valara hadn't a clue what her ladyship was referring to.

"Come, join me beside the fire. I have important matters to discuss before Sir Roger takes it in his head there is nothing for him here and hies back to Town."

"What can you mean?" Valara said, as she followed the dowager and settled down in front of a fire that had fallen to ashes.

Lady Margaret stared at her younger companion, as if taking her measure. "You do wish your cousin to be happy?"

"I do."

"Are *you* hoping for Westoke to make an offer, as Belinda is?"

Valara shook her head. "He is not a man who will make any wife happy, in my opinion. I know it is the custom for a girl to marry for wealth and position, but I—"

"A foolish custom in my opinion, my dear. But what does your cousin think of the man?"

There was a long silence as Valara pondered whether she could break the confidences she and her cousin held. There was no point in keeping a secret that would soon be known to all, for if the earl did offer, Ellie intended to refuse him. "She tells me she cannot like him."

"Excellent. Then my old eyes have not been deceiving me, for I have noted a certain look in Miss Addington's gaze when it rests on our handsome young baronet."

Valara's fingers traced the intricate carving of a lion head on the arm of one of the new chairs her ladyship had brought from London. "I won't deny I think she has feelings for Sir Roger, but there is Aunt Belinda to contend with."

"Nonsense, my dear. You let me handle the baroness. Besides, my godson holds the purse strings for the estate, which effectively negates Belinda's control over her daughter. You certainly don't think he would object to the girl making a match with his friend?"

Biting at her lip, Valara shook her head before she asked, "Do you think Sir Roger will make Ellie an offer?"

"Not as long as he thinks she intends to accept Westoke when his offer comes, which is what I believe he is thinking." The dowager sat back and waited for her statement to sink in.

Valara frowned. She occasionally questioned Ellie about the proposed match, but it was not a common topic in general. "Few people, save Aunt Belinda, ever mention the possibility of an offer these days, and she has been out of company since her accident."

"Unless I miss my guess, your brother told him the day they went to have a new coat made in Holt. Sir Roger has been as frosty as a winter pane to your cousin since then."

One couldn't blame him if he thought Ellie had been merely toying with him while she waited for a man with better expectations, but Valara knew that was far from the truth. She would have to explain to Elaina why Sir Roger had turned cool.

The rhythmic gait of cantering horses echoed in the room and Valara rose. "They are returned." She hurried to the door and waited until the gentlemen entered the Great Hall, then hurried across as they surrendered their hats, gloves, and crops to the footman. Her gaze was riveted on Lord Landry's face, which seemed an unreadable mask. "Is all well at Seaforth?"

His lordship nodded. "Have no fear. Mr. Binion is still in one piece and still running Seaforth."

Sir Roger took her hand. "We made certain there will be sufficient funds so that the vicar won't need to haunt the marshes at night."

Relief flooded Valara. She smiled at the baronet, thinking he had supplied that financial security. "Thank you." She looked to where her brother stood and found him quietly studying his nails. Something in his nonchalant stance was very strange. As her gaze roved from face to face and came to rest on Lord Landry's handsome countenance, she suddenly had the feeling that something was not being said.

Before Valara could question them further, Bainbridge stepped forward. "My lord, Cook has laid out a cold collation in the dining room for your nuncheon."

"Ladies," Lord Landry said, "do begin without us.

We shall join you once we have washed away our dirt and changed."

As Neville started past her, Valara clamped a hand on his sleeve and whispered, "Did something untoward happen at Seaforth?"

The boy's gaze followed the men as they strolled up the stairs. "Don't be ridiculous. Alexander handled everything like a regular Trojan. Had Binion confessing the whole, then eating out of his hand within minutes. Let go. I'm starved, and I cannot eat without changing."

Valara released her hold on her brother and watched him dash up the stairs. Something didn't feel right. She couldn't put her finger on what it was, but the gentlemen had been too—she searched for the right word— vague, that was it. There had been no details about how this matter had been accomplished so easily. Or were her nerves merely on edge because of tonight? Perhaps they would fill in the gaps during the simple repast they were about to share.

"Come, Valara, shall we go to the dining room?" Lady Margaret stood in the doorway of the drawing room, seemingly not at all interested in where the gentlemen had been.

Realizing that she had her own worries, namely making it safely to the mill and back this evening, Valara trailed along to have something to eat. She hoped Ellie would have some suggestions about how she could slip away tonight.

Conversation at the midday meal failed to provide any answers to Valara's questions about what had happened at Seaforth. All three gentlemen dawdled over their dressing and the ladies, joined by a subdued Elaina, had eaten their fill by the time the gentlemen arrived. Despite her worries about what the men might be keeping secret, Valara didn't fail to note the constraint between Elaina and Sir Roger. Lady Margaret might be correct about the baronet, but why was her cousin acting so strangely?

Elaina informed Lord Landry of Mr. Akers's visit and invitation to go sailing the next day. The matter was discussed, and all but Lady Margaret were agreeable to the scheme. A message would be sent confirming the arrangements.

Each time Valara attempted to turn the conversation to Mr. Binion, Lord Landry or Sir Roger interrupted to discuss estate business or inquire what the ladies plans were for the remainder of the day.

To her frustration, Lady Margaret rose to announce, "Ladies, come and allow the gentlemen to discuss their business. Lisette has set aside some time this afternoon to discuss the remainder of your wardrobes now that she has completed your evening gowns and habits. There is still a trunk full of fabric with which to fashion morning gowns, walking gowns, traveling gowns, and even ball gowns." The dowager lifted her lorgnette and raked each girl's drab apparel. "And there is not a moment to spare, from what I see."

Elaina's face lit. "My habit is ready?"

"Cecily was doing the hem when I stopped at the sewing room this morning."

Valara watched her cousin eagerly accompany the dowager to the door. There appeared to be no point in remaining behind, for it was apparent the gentlemen wouldn't discuss what had taken place at Seaforth. Valara was also extremely tired of the grim black wardrobe she had been forced to wear. She bid the gentlemen a pleasant day and hurried to catch up with the others.

The afternoon flew past as the ladies matched fabrics and trim with fashion plates. For a brief time, Valara was able to put aside Frenchmen, smugglers, her fears for her uncle, and even her thoughts about Lord Landry. She was inundated with discussions about cambrics and muslins, sleeves and bodices, ribbons, lace, and rouleaux.

At last, Lisette announced, *"Mademoiselles,* it ez time for you to dress for dinner, *hein?* You must look your best in your new gowns for zee gentlemen." The little seamstress beamed at the girls.

Elaina muttered, "As if they would even notice." She rose and thanked the Frenchwoman and her assistant before leaving. Valara added her thanks, then hurried after her cousin.

Remembering Elaina's cool treatment of the baronet at nuncheon, Valara fell into step with the girl. "Have you quarreled with Sir Roger?"

Elaina's expression became aloof. "I have no wish to discuss that gentleman. We have other things to worry about. Do you go to the mill tonight?"

"I must, but now that his lordship has unmasked Mr. Binion and put a stop to his operation, there should be little danger of running across anyone near the mill."

Elaina stopped and put her hand on her cousin's arm. "Then let me go with you. I promise I will only watch from the edge of the woods. I cannot think you should trust this Frenchman, and I want to be there if something should go wrong."

Thinking her cousin was merely wishing for a bit of adventure before Uncle Philippe returned and put an end to the escapade, Valara nodded. "I will let you come if you will allow me to tell you one thing I think you should know about Sir Roger."

A momentary look of hurt flashed across Elaina's face before she schooled her features to indifference. "Oh, very well, but I cannot think why I would want to hear anything about him. He didn't even have the manners to dance with me—er, I mean any of the ladies at Westwood last evening."

Valara crossed her arms. "That might be because he thought you preferred to dance with Lord Westoke."

Elaina's mouth opened as if she intended to say something, but no words came out.

"He knows about the late earl's and your father's wishes. I fear Nev might have given him the idea it was your wish, as well."

A look of horror filled the girl's face. "I won't marry that coxcomb, and so I told mother this morning."

"I think it is Sir Roger you should tell." Valara smiled as her cousin's face flushed pink.

"So I shall." She marched off down the hall, and Valara sighed. Why couldn't things be so easy for her? But then Alexander wasn't the wealthy grandson of a Cit.

A very determined young lady made her way downstairs, but to Elaina's disappointment, all three gentlemen had gone to inspect the work on the Dower House and had yet to return. Bainbridge informed her that dinner had been set back by one hour.

It was near seven o'clock when the gentlemen strode into the drawing room where the ladies awaited them. Lord Landry, handsome in a blue superfine coat over a white waistcoat and cream knee pants, bowed, saying, "Do forgive us, ladies, but Mr. Bailey insisted I approve some of the changes the carpenters suggested on the dower house. Shall we go in?"

He offered Lady Margaret his arm and the others followed.

Dinner proved to be surprisingly elaborate, with some six removes. Conversation was general and finally moved to the subject of Lord Landry's sisters and when they would visit. Her ladyship paused, a thoughtful expression on her face.

"By the by, what was in that small box Amy had me

send via the late baron's solicitor? Until this moment I had quite forgotten the matter."

The baron smiled, then tugged a gold chain and a medallion from beneath the starched collar at his throat. It lay atop his simply tied cravat, twinkling in the candlelight. "A good luck charm."

Valara recognized it as what she'd seen the night of Miss Crane's attack. "It is unusual. What is the picture etched on the front?"

Lord Landry quickly recounted the tale of buying the Minerva medallion, a talisman for wisdom and prudence, in Rome years earlier and giving it to Adriana with the admonition to pass it on to Amy once she'd found her heart's desire.

"It seems my little sister thought I could use a bit of luck."

Valara couldn't resist asking, "And do you think it has been lucky?"

The baron's amber gaze locked on her. "Without a doubt."

She suddenly felt warm all over, but the moment was lost when Neville interrupted, "You have no idea how lucky it has been. Why . . ."

His lordship frowned and the boy fell quiet. Lady Margaret covered the gaffe. "Why, it's a lovely charm, but I have found luck to be fickle and often in need of a helping hand."

Neville's brows rose, not taking her meaning. "Well, I don't believe in fuzzing dice or marking cards."

Elaina made a face at her cousin. "I believe he said it was to help his sisters find their heart's desire, not to win some silly game of chance."

His lordship rose, tossing his napkin to the table. "I assure you, Neville, it is merely a gold trinket with questionable magical powers. I wear it to remind me of my sisters, whom I have missed dearly." He looked about at the others. "Since we must be ready to leave for Mr. Akers's quay by eleven, I suggest we skip tea and make it an early night."

Valara's gaze flew to Elaina's face, and she could see the disappointment that there would be no time for a moment alone with Sir Roger. The ladies all rose and politely said their good nights while the baron, his friend, and Neville removed to the library for a 'bit of brandy,' as her brother informed Valara when she asked to speak with him. He told her he'd see her in the morning and strode off with the confidence of having been included by the older men.

Upstairs, Valara bid the waiting maid good night. After some thirty minutes, she pulled out her black gown and cloak and dressed for her trip to the mill. She slipped the money pouch into the pocket of her underskirt, then sat down to wait for the household to settle down for the night.

Was there any such thing as a true good luck charm? She doubted such, but obviously the Addington sisters believed the Minerva medallion's powers had helped them marry for love. Valara could only hope it would do the same for the baron, for she wouldn't wish a marriage of convenience on anyone.

Scarcely ten minutes after Valara sat down, her door opened. Elaina entered without a knock, shut the door behind her, and stood breathless, her head against the wood.

"Something very mysterious is going on."

"What do you mean?"

Elaina hurried across the room to the window, where the curtains had been drawn against the night. "Did you not say Alexander had put an end to Binion's smuggling?"

Valara rose. "That is what he said."

"Then why did he and Sir Roger just slip out the li-

brary doors, one going toward Cley and the other toward
the mill?" Elaina blew out the candles, then drew open
the curtains as Valara moved to where her cousin stood.

It took a moment for their eyes to adjust to the darkness. Both peered out the window. Valara could swear
she saw movement on the edge of the path that led to
the mill. Then it was gone. Why were the men out there
if it was all at an end? She stepped back and put a hand
to her stomach, which had suddenly tightened when
she thought of Alexander putting himself in danger.
"What does this mean?"

Ellie leaned against the windowpane as if she might
see better into the darkness. "It means it is going to be
very crowded on the marshes tonight, and you shall
need my help more than ever."

"Help? What do you intend to do?" Things were rapidly spiraling out of her control, to Valara's way of thinking.

"I must distract whichever one went to the mill while
you go and put the Frenchman's money in the box and
retrieve your uncle's message."

"How?"

"If it is Alexander, I suppose I could simply knock
him on the head. That would certainly make Mama
happy."

"Don't you dare." Valara was incensed at such an idea.

"I was only teasing. I shall find something to argue
about. We have never had trouble finding a topic to
quarrel about before." Then she grew quiet for a moment before adding, "And if it is Sir Roger, I shall very
likely kiss him. That should convince him I don't want
Westoke."

Before Valara could utter a word of protest at her
cousin's scandalous plan, Elaina grabbed her by the
arm and dragged her across the room. "Come. We
must hurry or the Frenchmen will be there before us.

You leave from the front and make your way round the edge of the field to the mill. I shall go straight through the woods."

Eleven

Crouched low, Valara crept the last twenty yards through the swaying grass to the mill. As she moved over the field, she struggled against the wind's constant effort to pull her hood from over her head. She knew from past experience her blond curls could give her away even on moonless nights. Every so often she thought she heard the murmur of voices on the wind and stopped to look furtively about, but she saw no one. She hoped Ellie had found the baron and was keeping him distracted as she'd promised when they parted at the edge of the woods. With any luck, Ellie might be able to lure whichever gentleman went toward the mill back to the Chase.

Her thoughts centered on Alexander, and she became curious why he and Sir Roger were out here. Were they still trying to rout out smugglers? Or had they decided to make a last run for Mr. Binion? She could see them volunteering to run such a risk to protect the boys, but she couldn't imagine two real gentlemen engaged in the trade. If they had, she prayed that Waite was nowhere around.

At last she reached the tower and pressed herself against the flint stones that jutted out unevenly, trying to keep from making herself a silhouette against the night sky. She edged around the building, stepping gingerly onto the gravel path in front of the door.

About to lift the sign plate that covered the hidden alcove, she stopped and moved to press her ear to the door, remembering her last time and the nasty surprise that had stepped from the doorway. There was no sound inside. She moved back and slowly lifted the mill's sign.

Without warning, a cold hand clamped round her neck and she involuntarily screamed. Something struck her from the rear. Then everything went black.

Alexander watched in silence from the edge of the woods as Binion and his boys led the small pack ponies loaded with casks back along the edge of the marsh. The drop had been made at Akers's Quay, and everything seemed to be going without incident. Even the sounds of the ponies' hooves were lost beneath the howl of the wind off the sea. Hopefully, Waite and his men were still watching the Dower House.

As the last of the loaded animals disappeared into the cluster of trees almost a mile down the shore to Alexander's left, a limb cracked and he spun round. His neck prickled as he raked the darkness for movement.

Suddenly Elaina stepped from the shadows. "Landry! What are you doing out here hiding in the trees?" she asked, in a contrary tone. She was barely visible, standing a few feet from him, her white face the only thing he could make out in the darkness.

"Why don't you speak a bit louder, Cousin? I don't think they heard you in Cley," he said through clenched teeth, grabbing her arm and drawing her into the inky blackness of the tree where he stood. "Are the ladies of the Chase trying to put a period to their existence by wandering about the estate after dark?"

"I came to see what you and your friend are about sending us all to bed, then slipping out of the house like . . . well, like you had business to transact on the marshes."

Alexander stiffened. "Are you accusing me of being in league with French smugglers?"

"There is the estate to repair and there is good money to be made, or so many men wouldn't take the risk. Did I not just see a line of men and ponies passing with contraband brandy? Are you their new leader now Binion has finished with the business?"

Still holding her arm, he gently shook her before she pulled free. "It is nice to know my own relations think so poorly of me, Cousin. But allow me to inform you that I don't need to risk dragging brandy over these marshes when I own two mills in Yorkshire. I am out here trying to keep that fool Binion or one of his boys from being killed while they complete their obligations to those French scoundrels who involved them."

She peered silently at the distant mill for a moment, tugging her cloak about her. "Well, if you aren't involved, let us return to the manor. I should like to know how it is that you have acquired your wealth on a soldier's earnings. Besides, it is too cold out here to be—"

A rustle of leaves sounded behind them, and Neville appeared though the trees. "What are *you* doing here, Ellie?"

"I might ask you the same thing," Alexander snapped. He hadn't wanted the boy out here exposed to danger. All he needed now was to have Lady Margaret and Valara appear to make his night a disaster.

"I came to tell you I saw my sister on the marshes heading for the mill. I know it was Lara because the wind caught her hood and exposed her blond hair for a moment." Neville moved to the edge of the trees and stared at the mill, but from the great distance and over-

whelming darkness, one could only see the large black
tower looming against the starry sky.

Alexander's stomach knotted. Valara was once again
out here risking her life. His gaze moved to his cousin's
shadowy figure. "What are you two about tonight? And
don't spin me any Banbury tale."

"What do you mean?" Elaina's tone was all innocence, but her face was cloaked in darkness and he
couldn't tell if she was dissembling.

Alexander took a step closer, his voice deadly quiet.
"Why has Valara been going to the mill at night?"

Neville returned to where his lordship was questioning his cousin, suddenly interested in news of which
he'd been unaware. "What is my sister doing out at
night? She hasn't involved herself with the Gentlemen
for my sake, has she?"

Elaina gave a brittle laugh. "You are both being quite
ridiculous. Lara is the good one, the respectable one.
Everyone says so. I am—"

A scream pierced the night. It came from the direction of the mill.

Elaina dashed to the edged of the trees and cried,
"Lara!"

Without questions, Alexander raced across the field
straight for the mill. He hadn't needed to be told the
cry had been Valara's. He didn't know what she was
involved with. All he knew was that she was in trouble
and needed him.

The distance between the mill and the edge of the
trees was nearly half a mile, but as fear tore at Alexander's insides, it seemed more like ten miles as he ran.
In the distance, he could barely make out several shadowy figures who seemed to be carrying something . . .
or someone . . . back toward the marsh. Then he discerned the outline of a small manned rowboat waiting

at the shore. Fear seared him as he realized Valara was being abducted.

As he rounded the mill, Alex saw the men lower the body they carried into the small rowboat and push off through the marsh until they reached the open water. Then they climbed in, and the companions who'd awaited them began to paddle.

Desperate to stop the abductors, but knowing the distance was still too great, he pulled a pistol from his pocket. "Halt or I shall fire!" he shouted as he rushed to the water, but his words seemed to be taken away on the wind. The men in the boat rowed harder, making for their vessel, which lay somewhere in the darkness beyond view.

Alex splashed through the marsh, heedless of the bitter cold water that got deeper and impeded him. Finally the grass gave way to open sea. He couldn't reach the boat. A feeling of rage overwhelmed him, and the waves battered him while he watched helplessly as the boat carrying Valara was swallowed by the night.

Wading back on shore, he found a breathless Elaina and Neville. "Who were they, Cousin?" Alex demanded. "And why would they want Miss Rochelle?"

The time for secrets was past. Elaina held back nothing. She explained about the Rochelle's uncle and his mission in France, about the messages being passed to London, and about Valara's final meeting with Dubois and his demand for money before the next message was delivered.

Neville fumed, "What could Uncle Philippe be thinking to involve Lara when I was here to handle things? I swear I'll kill him if anything happens to her." There was a catch in his voice as he added, "She's always taken care of me."

Alex peered up the beach, catching sight of several figures moving toward them through the darkness.

"There is no purpose to be gained by second guessing your uncle's decision. Our time would be better spent trying to find a way to recover your sister. Hold your tongue for now. We have visitors."

But the visitors proved to be Sir Roger and Danny come to inform them the brandy was safely out of their hands, awaiting the next group in the chain of smugglers. As the baronet noted Miss Addington had joined them, he asked, "What has happened?"

Alex quickly explained, then finished with, "We need a boat."

Neville pointed eastward. "Mr. Akers has the *White Gull* harbored over at his quay for our trip in the morning. It's a fast little sloop, and I know he'll gladly sail us anywhere."

The baron looked at the lad from Seaforth. "Danny, do you know where these men came from?"

"Me uncle says they're from a French village called Saint Pol. Said the whole lot is run by some flash-cove named Juneau that lives in a fancy house left by some Frenchies what lost their heads to the guillotine a long time ago."

"Good lad. Can you escort Miss Addington home and—"

"I won't go." Elaina took a step back. "I'm coming with you. Lara might need me."

Sir Roger snapped, "It's too dangerous."

Elaina walked up the shore toward the quay, calling over her shoulder, "I'm going, and that's final."

Alexander knew there was no time to argue. Valara was being taken further away with each minute that passed. "Very well. We must hurry."

Sprinkles of cold water fell on Valara's face, bringing her back to consciousness. The rhythmic splash of oars in water was the first sound she became aware of. Her head ached dreadfully. She was cold and feeling a bit sick. She opened her eyes and realized her hands were tied, and she lay in the bottom of a leaky boat that stunk of fish and seawater. Despite being dazed, her memory of being at the mill returned, and she quickly realized Dubois had struck her and intended to take her to France for some unknown reason.

As her thoughts became more ordered, she could see the Frenchman's profile in the bow as he turned to look back at the shore. He barked orders in French to his men to row harder; someone was pursuing them.

With an effort, she struggled to sit up. One of the other smugglers called a warning to their leader and pushed her back down. Dubois merely turned his head in her direction, but his face was a black void in the night, giving her no idea what he was thinking. He made no comment, only appeared to stare.

Determined to keep her wits about her, she cried, "*Monsieur,* what is the meaning of this outrage? I brought you the money you demanded. Where is the message you were to bring? Why are you abducting me?"

"Who ez Jacques Montaine, *mademoiselle?*"

Valara's heart skipped a beat. Clearly they were suspicious of her uncle, but why? "Wh-what do you mean? You know who he is. He is the man I love."

"Zen you will be pleased to know zat you will soon be reunited with your lover."

Even with tremors of fear surging through her, Valara managed to keep her voice calm. "Then you are taking me to France. I am happy I shall see my dear Jacques again."

"*Oui,* but will he be happy to see you, *mademoiselle?*"

Valara knew her uncle wouldn't be, for she only made him more vulnerable to whatever plot the Frenchman was involved with. She lay back, closing her eyes, and prayed that Elaina and the baron had heard her scream. They were her only hope.

It was just after midnight when the butler at Akers's Roost answered the persistent knocking at the door. Behind him, his master stood on the stairs, a dueling pistol in his hand, for one rarely got visitors this late at such a remote estate. When the door opened to reveal Landry and the others, the gentleman's brows rose in surprise and his gaze roved to the clock. "There seems to be some mistake, Lord Landry. I meant to take you sailing at twelve noon, not twelve midnight."

The baron stepped into the light of the candles. "Akers, we need the *White Gull*. Miss Rochelle was abducted by French smugglers and is being taken to Saint Pol."

Mr. Akers was no fool and wasted no time asking questions. He immediately began to bark orders at the butler for men, supplies, and clothes to be made ready. As the servant hurried off, he turned back to Landry. "Await me on the quay. I should be able to set sail within fifteen minutes."

After the gentleman hurried up the stairs, Alexander requested pen and paper to write a note to be sent to the Chase, informing the ladies of their sudden trip. Handing it to a footman with the request that it be delivered in the morning, the baron and the others made their way to the stone quay. Silence reigned as they stared out at the *White Gull* anchored just offshore, each with his own thoughts about Valara's peril.

Alexander prayed they would find her safe and unharmed. A wave of nausea tickled the back of his throat as the possibilities of what such brutes might do to a beautiful young woman careened through his mind. Such thoughts were so paralyzing he reminded himself that this had something to do with her uncle and his mission in France. They wouldn't hurt her—at least until they got back to the *comte*.

As good as his word, Mr. Akers appeared in time. Within ten minutes, the sails of the *White Gull* were filling with wind, drawing the ship and its anxious passengers south.

Standing beside the man as he guided his vessel and called orders to his small crew, Alexander asked, "Can we overtake them before they reach France?"

Akers was quiet a moment, then shrugged. "There is always a chance, but I have no idea what kind of vessel they are sailing. By first light, the channel will be full of ships and we don't want to have to board them all. It would be better to sail straight for this Saint Pol." He gave a slight grin. "I consider myself a damned fine sailor. Who knows? With luck and good winds, we might even beat the blackguards there."

"How long will it take?" Alexander prayed the man's skills were as good as he claimed.

"Twelve to eighteen hours, depending on the weather. You and the others might want to go below and to try to sleep."

Alexander feared he might go mad with so much time before he would see Valara again. He knew he'd never be able to close his eyes. His thoughts kept returning to what might be happening to her.

A hand clapped on his shoulder, and Sir Roger drew him away from Akers. "Come. You won't be any good to her if you are weak from exhaustion."

His friend was correct. With a last look at the dark horizon, Alexander followed his friend below, knowing there was little he could do. Elaina trailed behind. The gentlemen insisted she take Akers's cabin. They would use the smaller ones.

After Alex disappeared into a room across the way,

Elaina stepped closer to speak with Sir Roger. Before she could utter a word, he snapped, "You shouldn't have come. It's too dangerous, and you are more likely to get yourself or someone else killed than to be of any help." He turned his back and entered the cabin, closing the door with a marked bang.

Frustrated, Elaina wanted to scream until Roger came back to her. But she would not be so selfish. This was not the time to end the misunderstanding with the man she knew she'd come to love. Her first concern must be for Lara.

It proved to be a long night for everyone on board the *White Gull*.

Valara shielded her eyes from the light when the door to her dark cell opened. It had been hours since she been taken below deck and locked in the small room with a foul-smelling bunk against walls that leaked seawater. When two sailors dragged her to her feet and out the door, she thought her knees would buckle. She'd been quite ill during the rough crossing, but after the first few steps she found her strength.

The men hauled her up on deck, where no one seemed particularly interested in her as the crew went about the business of stowing sails and ropes. At last, adjusting to the brightness of the late afternoon sun, Valara was a bit disappointed at her first look at the land of her ancestors. The French town appeared much like any small fishing village in England, with whitewashed houses lining the piers, fishing nets strung out to dry or be repaired, and ordinary men and women going about their business.

The two sailors released her and left her standing alone in the middle of the main deck. As the sun sank lower, she realized she'd been a prisoner for nearly a day. Was anyone searching for her? Putting that disturbing worry aside, she moved to the rail and looked about.

Everyone seemed to be hurrying away from the wharf as the sun sank lower. She suddenly wondered how difficult it would be to escape. Were all the residents in league with Dubois and his men? If she did escape, should she search for Uncle Philippe or try to find a way back across the channel to Landry Chase?

"Ah, *mademoiselle.*" Dubios's hated voice spoke behind her, interrupting her musing. "You are anxious to go and see your lover, *non?*"

She turned to see Dubois for the first time in the light of day. There was little improvement. Greasy brown hair hung from beneath a battered red beret. His skin was pockmarked and leathery, and his few remaining teeth were stained, making his age indeterminate. His clothing looked as if it hadn't seen soap and water since Twelfth Night.

Trying to keep her wits, she pasted a smile on her face. "But of course I am."

He lifted his hands, displaying leather straps across his palms. "Must I tie you, or will you give zee promise not to try and escape?"

Lifting her chin, she sneered, "I don't know what game you are playing, *monsieur,* but I am determined to see Jacques. He will put this charade to an end."

"We shall see," he said, returning the leather ties to his pocket, then gesturing her to come with him. Within minutes, she was seated alone in an ancient coach rumbling away from the village. She peered out at the passing countryside, wondering if someone, anyone from the Chase would come after her.

A chill ran down her spine. Did they even know where to come? It was a daunting thought, but she reminded herself Elaina had been somewhere in the nearby woods, and she would surely have gotten help. Would

Alexander be willing to come so far for someone who hadn't been forthcoming in her dealings with him? She'd been a fool.

Her thoughts returned to their meeting in the hall that very morning. Had he not called her *cara?* The look in his eyes had made her pulse race, and she knew in her heart he would come, but would he be in time?

A few minutes later, the carriage rumbled onto a cobblestone drive. She peered out the window and could see rusted gates hanging askew and an abandoned gatehouse as they passed onto the grounds of a French estate. Somehow she couldn't imagine smugglers being involved with a man of consequence, but then Mr. Binion's involvement had stunned her as well.

The carriage drew to a halt and the door was soon jerked opened by Dubois. "Welcome to zee chateau, *mademoiselle.*"

She climbed down in front of a beautiful old building covered in ivy. It owned an abandoned air with its darkened windows and overgrown shrubs. There were no footmen at the door, only a lantern with grimy glass that muted the light.

Dubois roughly grabbed her arm and hauled her into the main hall, where a few candles illuminated the large foyer, leaving much of the room in deep shadows. Debris lay about the floor, and paintings as well as tapestries hung askew or were missing. It was sad to see the interior in worse condition than the outside, but what it really needed most was a good cleaning. There could be little doubt the chateau was some kind of meeting place and not the actual home of anyone. What could have happened to the family who had once lived here? Then she remembered that the Reign of Terror had eradicated many noble families.

The Frenchman marched her down a hall and threw open a door to a drawing room on the first floor. Unlike the rest of what she'd seen, this room was in reasonably good condition, with pale blue walls and worn blue damask sofas. Her gaze riveted on the back of a tall gentleman who stood facing the fireplace.

In rapid French, Dubois announced he had returned with Montaine's lady.

The gentleman turned and smiled at her, but there was such menace in his dark eyes that a chill raced down her spine.

"Welcome to my chateau, *mademoiselle*. I am Claude Juneau, your host."

Valara made no response as Dubois shoved her into a chair that faced her captor. The man was tall and near fifty, she would guess, with black hair graying at the temples. He had a straight nose and full, well-shaped mouth, but deep groves were etched in his brow, as if frowning were his common expression. One might once have called him handsome before life had hardened those refined features.

Fear gripped Valara as he moved to stand beside her chair. He used a finger to lift her chin and survey her as one might a painting. "Strange, *mademoiselle*, but you bear a remarkable resemble to the one who claims you as his *Anglais* lover."

Pulling her chin free, she sneered, *"Monsieur,* blue eyes and blond hair are quite common in England. Where is Monsieur Montaine?"

Doubt remained in the shadows reflected in his eyes, but he looked back at the smuggler. "Dubois, bring Jacques." Returning his intense gaze to her, he asked, "What ez your name?"

Her thoughts in a whirl, Valara knew her own French name would be her uncle's undoing at once. She didn't know what her uncle might have said to this man, so she merely used the more English version of her own name that the family had always used. "Lara."

Juneau moved back to the fire. Drawing his hands behind his back, he began to interrogate her. He hurled questions at her about her, her uncle, and the man's life in Paris. She answered only those about herself, pretending ignorance about Montaine and all connected with him. In truth, she knew little of her uncle's activities..

To her relief, the door opened and Uncle Philippe stepped into the room, followed by Dubois. The *comte* looked haggard and defeated, his clothes rumpled, his shoulders sagging, his graying blond hair in matted tufts. Then horror etched his face as his gaze lit on his niece. *"Mon dieu,* Lara."

She jumped to her feet and dashed across the room, throwing herself into his arms. "Jacques, my dear Jacques, what have they done to you?"

He crushed her in an embrace, whispering in her ear in French, "I'm sorry for endangering you, little one. Be brave."

They drew back and their blue gazes locked. A message of determination to survive passed between niece and uncle. The comte drew her into the curve of his arm and glared at Juneau. "Why have you brought Lara here?"

The Frenchman gestured them forward, and Dubois poked Philippe in the back, forcing them deeper into the room. The *comte* led his niece back to the chair where she had been and then stood beside her as they faced the leader of the smuggling ring.

Without warning, Juneau pulled a long dagger from his waist and stepped to Valara, putting the point at her throat. Speaking in French, he directed his questions to the man he knew as Montaine. "Perhaps now you will tell me why you do not marry your own true love instead of sending her letters. Why are you always conveniently elsewhere on the nights that the men must sail for the English coast?"

Philippe licked his lips. The truth was a death warrant. "I did not wish to bring her here where there is danger. Too many of our compatriots have already been arrested."

Valara winced as Juneau pressed the blade deeper and blood trickled down her neck. For the first time, she realized that she might never see Landry Chase again, that her dear Alexander might be too late to save her and Philippe.

"Do you take me for a fool? I soon began to realize that on the trips Dubois carried one of your billets-doux to *mademoiselle*, some loyal Bonapartist soon disappeared, never to be heard from again. I think you are betraying us and Napoleon." He reached in his pocket, pulled out a crumpled piece of paper, and shoved it into Philippe's face. "I became curious. Do you always communicate with women in code, Montaine?"

The *comte* snatched the letter, then glared at Dubois. "I was merely being cautious. Her parents might find one of the letters. Of course they were in code."

Juneau's eyes narrowed as he looked from one face to the other. "I do not trust you. We can do without the money you have provided. I think you and your lovely companion have betrayed our cause." He drew the knife away from Valara's throat and lowered it to just above her heart, giving an evil grin. "The punishment for you both shall be death."

Before his words and action had time to sink into Valara's stunned brain, the door to the drawing room burst open and the room filled with men—Englishmen.

"The only one to die here tonight, Juneau, is you, unless you stand away from Miss Rochelle." Alexander's voice held deadly intent, and he stood with his dueling pistol aimed directly at Juneau's chest.

Valara's gaze was locked on the blade that glinted

before her. As it moved backward slightly before its deadly plunge, she closed her eyes and prayed. The report of the gunshot in the drawing room was deafening. In the moment of silence following the blast, a body fell to the floor. There was a clamor of excited voices, but only one drew her attention.

"Mia amore, are you unharmed?"

Valara's eyes opened to the wonderful sight of an unshaven Alexander standing in a cloud of gun smoke, concern carved on his face.

She flew into to his arms. "You came! But how did—"

He crushed her to him, silencing her with a demanding kiss. For a brief time nothing existed in the world except the two of them and raw emotion. At last he drew back, and in a husky voice asked, "Are you unharmed, *mia dolcezza?*" Then he saw the wound on her neck and pulled a handkerchief from his coat and blotted the blood. "You are hurt."

"It is nothing, only a prick." She wondered what the endearment meant, but merely placed her head to his chest. "How did you find us?" Juneau lay on the floor, unconscious and bleeding from a shoulder wound. Neville held a pistol trained on him.

Alexander swept his arm to his left, where the remainder of his rescue team stood clustered near the door, allowing the pair a modicum of privacy. "We are here thanks to Mr. Akers's superior sailing skills. We also owe Danny for telling us who ran this ring of blackguards. Then there was Neville's ability to speak perfect French to help us find where this Dubois would take you, and thanks to Elaina, who told us what this had all been about."

"Thank you, all. You cannot know how frightened I was." She looked up into Alexander's eyes. "I knew you would come. Can you forgive me for not telling you about my uncle? For putting you all to such trouble?"

She looked to where Mr. Akers, her cousin, and Sir Roger stood just inside the doorway, while Danny held Dubois, keeping him from escaping.

Alex tilted her chin upward. "I suppose I can understand why you didn't trust a stranger, especially one whose name you had heard blackened for years." He kissed her on the lips, then turned to face the older gentleman, who was frowning behind Valara's chair.

"Comte Ouelette, I presume." Alexander extended his hand. "I am Landry, of Landry Chase, and wish to request your permission to pay my addresses to your niece." Then he looked back at Valara. "If she will have me."

Ouelette crossed his arms, looking at the young man who'd saved their lives. He seemed to like what he saw, for at last he extended his hand. "I'm glad to hear your intentions are honorable, since I'm too old to be standing at twenty paces with Hugh's son. But, my boy, you'd best know Valara, Neville, and I haven't a feather to fly with, as you *Anglais* say. I have expectations of reward for my services from Louis, but for zee moment our pockets are to let."

Alex grinned at the *comte*. "I have no need of your money, Ouelette. I want only your niece."

Valara's heart pounded with exhilaration that Alexander wanted to marry her, but then reality hit her like a splash of cold water. He would be sacrificing all his plans for the Chase by marrying her. His decision didn't just affect her, but all those who depended on the estate for their livelihood. Knowing it was the most painful thing she'd ever done, she put her hand on his arm. "I-I cannot marry you." She rushed from the room.

Alexander barked, "See to these two villains, Roger. I shall return in a moment with my betrothed."

Ouelette made as if to follow, but Sir Roger stopped him.

"I won't let Landry force my niece into marriage if she does not wish it." The older man glowered at the younger.

"He won't, sir." Elaina spoke up. "I think they will be quite happy together." Then she turned to Sir Roger. "I suppose I shall have to be abducted before you will admit your feelings, as well."

The baronet's eyes widened. "But I thought . . ." He hesitated. Then, seeing the look in her eyes, he smiled.

Elaina threw her arms around the gentleman's neck. "Don't think. Just kiss me."

Sir Roger held her off for a moment. "I won't abandon my grandfather."

"I would never ask you to, my love. Will you marry me?" To Ouelette's utter disgust, they made quite a spectacle of themselves, oblivious to the embarrassment of the observers.

The *comte* turned to Neville and in French asked, "What I should like to know is where is your aunt Belinda? I would never have left Valara with her had I known she would allow the girls to behave in such an outrageous manner—to be throwing themselves into the arms of the nearest man at a moment's notice."

Neville grinned and replied in the same language, "They have been quite a pair tonight. Don't surprise me about Ellie, but I didn't think Lara had it in her." Then his face fell. "Aunt Belinda ain't going to be well pleased."

Akers shrugged, joining the conversation in slightly accented French. "Not much does please that old harridan."

Ouelette's brows rose. "I had quite forgotten what a squeeze-crab the old dragon was. I guess I cannot blame the girls for wanting to be out from under her thumb. We shall allow the gentlemen the girls have chosen to worry about their conduct henceforth. Shall we have some brandy while we wait?" The older man walked to a nearby table and poured out three generous portions, then looked at Miss Addington and the fellow who had her in his arms. When he realized they weren't interested, he put the decanter down. He carried a glass to Akers and another to Neville, then lifted his in toast. "Here's to happy endings."

Outside, Alexander found Valara standing at a weed-choked fountain in front of the chateau, her arms wrapped about her to ward off the chill. He spun her around, and from the light of the lone lantern at the door, he could see tears glistening on her face.

Cupping her face with his hands, he asked, "Do you love me, *mia dolcezza*?"

"I—I cannot ask you to sacrifice all that Landry Chase could be for me. You need an heiress."

He kissed away the tears, then smiled. "I need you. I want you. I love you." He kissed her mouth, erasing any doubts she might have had. At last he drew back as they stared raptly at one another, both a bit breathless. "You must not always believe what the gossips say, *dolcezza*. Thanks to Sir Roger's grandfather, I have all the blunt I shall ever need. Marry me and make me the happiest of men—unless you cannot like that my funds have come from trade as, no doubt, will Aunt Belinda."

"You are wealthy? You don't need to marry an heiress?" Valara couldn't believe her ears. Might her dreams come true?

"I'm no Golden Ball, but I certainly shall have enough to do everything I want to Landry Chase and still afford a wife."

She melted into his arms. "I love you and, yes, I will marry you."

Another ten minutes passed before the lovers remembered that the others awaited them in the chateau. They arrived to find Elaina in Sir Roger's arms, a glow on her face. "Wish me happy, Cousins. Sir Roger has accepted my offer of marriage."

The baronet grinned at her. "Saucy minx."

After Alexander announced their betrothal and all had given their best wishes, they decided it was time to do something about Juneau and Dubois. Ouelette volunteered for that duty. He suggested that the others retire to the inn in Saint Pol and he would join them there later. Several hours later, a tired but happy group settled in for the night.

In the morning, the *comte* stood on the docks waving good-bye as Akers's small sloop set sail. He'd promised to come for the wedding of his niece once he'd been to Paris to inform them that his operation was at an end and give them the names of the remaining conspirators.

Alexander and Valara remained at the rail the longest. When the small French town was no longer discernable he said, "I have a request, *mia dolcezza.*"

"What is that you call me?" Valara looked up at the face she adored.

He kissed her mouth. "Sweetness, which is how you taste, *cara.*"

She laughed. "What is your request?"

"That we marry the first week in May so my sisters might come."

She bit her lip. "Do you think they shall like me?"

"They will adore you, as do I." Alex then proceeded to show his betrothed just that.

Epilogue

Lady Margaret turned her head and listened. "I think they are returned at last." She looked across and smiled at Miss Crane, who sat petting Boris's wiry head.

Minutes later, the door to the green drawing room opened and the tired, rumpled travelers strolled in. Alexander, his arm around Valara, entered the room and casually greeted the ladies as if he were returning from a walk in the garden. Sir Roger, hand in hand with Elaina, came to their side. Neville went straight to the tea tray and began to devour biscuits and cake.

Landry, surprised to see Nora still at the Chase, enquired about Miss Crane's health.

"I am completely recovered, sir." The young lady blushed.

Lady Margaret patted the girl's hand. "We have had our bit of excitement here while you have been gallivanting heaven knows where."

Alexander smiled. "Tell us."

"It seems Lady Blythe took exception to her companion leaving her in the lurch, as she called it. Why, she accused this poor dear of throwing herself at you and claimed that was why she was outside and got attacked. She packed Nora's belongings and had them delivered here the morning your note arrived, informing her they were done with her at Westwood and were informing her father of her fast conduct on their way to London." Even as Lady Margaret told her tale, her wise old eyes were taking in the intimacy of her godson and Valara as well as that of the baronet and Miss Addington. "So I wrote a letter to Nora's father informing him what really happened and asking his permission for her to be my companion in London for the remainder of the Season."

Alexander smiled. "I had little doubt you could handle things in my absence, dear Lady Margaret."

The lady looked askance at him. "Well, you would have doubted your judgment had you seen us when Lady Landry learned of her daughter's disappearance. Her hysterics were endless, for she was convinced the lot of you were for Gretna Green. It took my boxing her ears to convince her otherwise. Do tell me I have not lied to her and now must apologize."

Alexander looked down into Valara's eyes, and there could be little doubt about the love in their faces. "You have not, but I fear my aunt shall be no less pleased with the news we bring her. Valara has consented to be my wife, and Elaina is betrothed to Sir Roger."

"Excellent, dear boy, but we are anxious to know where the five of you have been for the past three days. Your note was a bit vague, to say the least."

"France." Neville boasted, biscuit crumbs falling down the front of his coat. "Saving Uncle Philippe and Lara."

Alexander, seeing the stunned look on the ladies' faces, said, "Pray allow me to explain." He quickly went through Valara's aid to her uncle, then her abduction. He told of their use of Akers's sloop to follow and their rescue of her and the *comte*.

"Quite an adventure, but all has ended well." Her ladyship rose and kissed each of the young ladies on the cheek. "May I wish you both happy? Pray let me know what I might do to be of assistance both now and in preparation for the weddings."

Elaina bit at her lip, then looked from Sir Roger to the dowager. "We could use your help when we tell Mama I intend to marry Roger."

Lady Margaret beamed. "But of course, my dear. I should like nothing better than to box your mama's ears again." She led the couple from the room, with Miss Crane and Boris trailing behind.

Neville's eyes twinkled. "I think I should like to see this." He hurried out of the room, but not before grabbing another handful of biscuits.

Valara's brows flattened into a frown. "You don't think she will actually do that, do you?"

Alexander turned and drew his future wife into an embrace. "I don't think she will need to. Elaina is of age and does not need her mother's consent. Besides, I think Lady Margaret could convince anyone that up was down and down was up if she set her mind to the matter."

Valara laughed, then surrendered to Alexander's wonderful kisses.

The wedding of Baron Landry and Miss Valara Rochelle took place on a beautiful spring morning the first week of May in the church at Cley. The vows were administered by the Right Reverend Montague Hart, Lord Bishop of Yorkshire and an old friend of Lady Margaret's.

The bride was resplendent in yards of white lace and silk, a lovely Minerva medallion about her neck. The groom was handsome in black coat, white waistcoat, and cream knee pants. Most of the village turned out to see the new baron and his lady wife.

The wedding proved to be something of a family re-

union, with Lord and Lady Borland recently returned
from Italy, Sir Hartley and Lady Ross back from Scotland, and the Comte Ouelette just arrived from France.
Earlier the *comte* had informed his niece and nephew
that King Louis had gifted him with the chateau at Saint
Pol and an ample reward to return him to the life of a
gentleman of means. Sir Roger and Lady Howard at-
tended the ceremony, having been married in a quiet
ceremony in London the previous week with Mr. Hull
in attendance.

The only person conspicuously absent was the dowager, Lady Landry. After numerous tears, a great deal of
ranting, and another sound boxing of her ears by Lady
Margaret, the baroness agreed to allow the baron to
purchase a house in London for her and to provide a
competence that would allow her to return to Society,
which had been her fondest wish. Most suspected she
would make her peace with her daughter's choice once
there was a grandchild to soothe her disappointment.

After the ceremony and a sumptuous meal back at
the Chase, the guests quickly departed, for the bride
and groom had decided to delay their honeymoon trip
until the state of the Chase was a bit more back to normal. The Borlands, the Rosses, Lady Margaret, and Miss
Crane left for Borland Abbey in York. Comte Ouelette
took his nephew and heir, Neville, back to France, saying the boy would be a great help while restoring Chateau Ouelette.

That evening, alone at the Chase but for the servants,
Alexander entered his wife's chamber for the first time.
He discovered her before a large open window. Her
blond hair lay loose about her shoulders. She was
dressed in a diaphanous blue nightrail and was staring
out at the marshes. The sheer material revealed her
feminine curves. His pulse quickened as he moved forward and slid his arms round her.

Without turning, she asked, "Do you think the smuggling on the estate is at an end?"

Alexander kissed the top of her head. "For the time being, now that Juneau and his men are imprisoned in Paris. I fear Captain Waite will spend many a night roving these beaches over the next few months without success."

She turned, pressing her warm body against her husband, looking up at him. He noted the Minerva medallion he'd given her lay in the valley of her breasts. Lifting the charm a moment, he said, "I don't think this should be called a good luck charm, but a wedding charm. It helped all my family find wedded bliss."

"After tonight, shall we store the medallion until our firstborn comes of age so he or she might find their heart's desire and wed for true love?"

Alex untied the ribbon of the blue gown. It slipped from Valara's shoulders to a heap on the floor. He took his love in his arms and kissed her soundly before he whispered, *"Dolcezza*, shall we see about making that firstborn?"

"Yes, please."

And so they did.

ABOUT THE AUTHOR

Lynn Collum lives with her family in Florida. She is the author of seven Zebra Regency romances and is currently working on her eighth, which will be published in 2002. Lynn loves hearing from readers. You may write to her c/o Zebra Books. Please include a self-addressed stamped envelope if you wish a response.